M000019587

PRAISE FOR CHARLES B. NEFF'S NOVELS

"It's all here in this story: love, decency and old, bone-crunching evil. Neff weaves them together brilliantly in a memorable page turner." Roger Wilkins, Pulitzer Prize winner

"... an intriguing and entertaining read, highly recommended." Midwest Book Review

"Neff used his substantial depth of knowledge and experience well, to draw the reader into a vivid image about life and just how easy it is for the power of evil to enter at any time." *The Cuckleburr Times*

"I admire writing that doesn't resort to frills and flowers to fill space. Just build the characters and tell the story. The author does that very well." Patricia Stoltey

"Keeps the reader fascinated and supremely entertained. Neff knows his business. This is a terrific read!" Grady Harp, 2012

"Charlie Neff gets better each time." C. Harald Hille

"Readers of Neff's delicious book will garner an exciting view of other lives." Ernst Schoen-René

"... another gripping page-turner by Charles Neff." Shannon Farley

"A swift timeline and memorable characters ... genuinely fascinating, intriguing and exciting." Sheila Deeth

"Don't start this book after noon – you won't be able to get to bed." Julius H. Anderson

"... holds the reader's interest from start to end, inspires and uplifts even as it threatens, and leaves its characters lingering in the mind long after the reading's done." Sheila Deeth

Also by Charles B. Neff

Fractured Legacy, 2014

Dire Salvation, 2012

Hard Cache, 2010

Peace Corpse, 2008

Patriot Schemes, 2006

Hidden Impact, 2004

SECOND GROWTH

by
Charles B. Neff

For Harry,

Thanks for the help!

Charlie

Copyright 2017 Charles B. Neff

All rights reserved. No part of this book may be reproduced or transmitted in any form by any means, electronic or mechanical, including photocopying and recording, or by any information storage and retrieval system, except as may be expressly permitted by the 1976 Copyright Act or the publisher. Requests for permission should be made in writing to: Bennett & Hastings Publishing, c/o the address posted at www.bennetthastings.com.

This is a work of fiction. All of the characters, names, incidents, organizations, and dialogue in this novel are either the products of the author's imagination or are used fictitiously. Bennett & Hastings titles may be ordered through booksellers or by contacting: sales@bennetthastings.com.

Library of Congress Control Number:
ISBN: 978-1-934733-93-6
Edited by Adam Finley

SECOND GROWTH

In the following pages you will meet:

Key Flanerty, nightclub employee, blogger

Crash Davies, educated drifter

Gary Seasons, state employee, former professional football player

Laura Dickens, state employee, MBA

Walt Vickers, Former CEO, Aerosteel Corporation

Curt Longcart, owner of Longcart Motors

Suzanne Bickers, actress

Bill McHugh, policeman from Swiftwater, WA

Clif Lerman, Longcart Motors employee

Flora Hayes, childhood friend of Key

Jim Purgis, plant manager, Aerosteel Corporation

Jeff Winter, legislative aide

Rick Groff, forester

Derek Bowman, Iraq War veteran

Rory Edwards, former accountant at Longcart Motors

Grant Tomson, Seattle investor and developer

OCTOBER 31

Grant Tomson observed the face in the mirror, still not able to get used to the fact that it was his own. His black hair hadn't lost its sheen, and his dark brown eyes, almost black from some angles, looked back with the haughty detachment he'd taught them to reflect. The beard was another matter. Gray was creeping in too early for a super-fit man who hadn't yet reached the downside of 40. If he were back in Seattle, he would have shaved it off, or at least dyed the offending bristles.

But he wasn't in Seattle. After his brother's death and some official suspicion that he'd been involved, he recognized that his public presence needed a vacation. He could have holed up in his penthouse apartment but chose instead to disappear entirely for a few months. That decision gave him a double reward: temporary isolation from the daily pressures of the business world, plus a thumb in the eyes of media outlets who felt robbed of the opportunity to keep up a drumbeat story about him. The disputed legacy of his lake property and the speculation about his brother's death had both faded as topics of public lust.

The cabin, 150 miles northeast of Seattle, was adequate. It belonged to one of his occasional employees, a man who brought him food and other supplies, and who appreciated what would happen to him if he told anyone where his boss was staying. His hide-out was the opposite of luxury, but well-enough built and insulated, with a reliable generator so he could count on wi-fi to keep him connected to his Seattle office most of the time. Only one person there, plus one other elsewhere, received his calls and knew how to reach him.

Boredom was his biggest enemy. He had books as an escape, and could go for long hikes to keep himself in shape. But they were not enough.

Had he stayed in Seattle, he would have had trouble anyway making new business deals until public memories about his past were erased. Meanwhile, his next play was well underway. Not much more could be done about it until some political issues were sorted out.

For the moment he needed to concentrate on what he'd always had trouble with: being patient. He'd just have to suck it up. But not without keeping close tabs on one loose end.

A tape recording made eight years ago was still out there. He'd left it alone until internet traffic gave him a hunch where it might be. By process of elimination, the hunch had grown to near certainty.

He'd be patient in every other way, but not about the location of that tape and how to get his hands on it.

Now.

※ ※ ※

Midnight. Key Flanerty caught herself in mid-stride, doused her flashlight, and dropped into a crouch against the low growth at the edge of the trail. On this late October night, the temperature had dropped into the mid-forties, and she fleetingly wished for the light jacket she'd left at home. Her eyes didn't adjust right away to the sudden darkness, and when a branch cracked nearby, it sounded like a gunshot. Her heart was a bass drum in her ears, and pressure built in her lungs. She fought against the cry that would burst out if she wasn't strong enough.

She had no other defense than to listen. Knowing the location of a stalker would be her only edge. When she could no longer hold it, she let her breath out gradually, small amounts passing pursed lips. Another wait and then a little more, until she heard only gusts of wind in the firs and the occasional vehicle climbing or descending in the night. The street they were on was hidden behind a thick wall of trees, but she could visualize its path up from the Sound, past the AlkiSteel mill, past homes and apartment buildings to the junction area of West Seattle.

It's Halloween, she suddenly remembered. She'd seen reminders everywhere on the way home—lighted yard decorations and, even at that late hour, some teenagers still on the streets in costume. But that fake spooky shit had nothing to do with her mood. Her imagination sometimes had a life of its own.

The rest of her brain began to work and she allowed first the possibility, then the probability, that what she heard was only a branch breaking off in the wind. She saw those dry branches each time she passed through this rare remnant of the forest that had once been here. This whole area would have looked like the woods where she grew up. She knew all about forests and their noises, and still her immediate reaction had been that someone was out there, looking for her.

Why? Could it be the old tape, the one her father gave her? For the past couple of years she'd gradually forgotten about it. Then, over the last two weeks, she thought she'd seen faces that stared at her a little too long. Or a shadow that stayed still and then moved away furtively. She'd given those signs only passing attention, figuring she was tired and must be imagining things. But maybe not. Her fear could also be a delayed reaction to hearing about her dad's death a month ago. She'd been away from him for almost four years. Suppose someone had finally forced him to reveal the existence of the tape, and now they were hunting her?

She rose and cautiously moved along the trail. Few people even knew this path existed. It snaked around the bases of medium-sized evergreens and exited into an overgrown clearing with a dark, almost formless shape at its center. Steps led up to a door. She opened the double locks with two different keys, yet hesitated about going in. Her inner voice was speaking again: You've forgotten to be careful. You've gotten soft.

She sat on a small bench by the door and concentrated on what else she might hear. Was it time to run again?

That's what she'd always done. It was the only dependable defense. Even as a small girl she'd learned to run into the woods when her six older brothers started a teasing game that soon turned to dangerous roughhousing. She was by far the smallest, but no one looked out for her. Okay, her father did, but he was gone most of the time. Her mother couldn't care less. Never did, never would. Her friend Flora cared and understood. Not that she could help; she had problems of her own.

Then her dad had put her in danger by entrusting that tape to her. So running away had been the only answer. She moved here to Seattle, and she got used to being safe. But she might be dangerously wrong.

And, she realized, her father hadn't explained everything. All he said was that a new logging job had come up, and someone wanted him to work on it, but he wouldn't—not after what had happened "the last time." She pressed him, but he refused to say more. By then he'd been out of work for two years, and times had been hard for the family. In the end, he'd given her the tape, told her to guard it, and all but pushed her out the door.

She knew he really didn't want to do that. He was the only person in her life who was close to her, the only person whose orders she would follow without question. She'd never traveled far from her rural home town before and, where Bellingham seemed large, Seattle was huge and overwhelming. At first she'd depended on instinct for protection. But instinct turned to habit, and habit gradually took her farther and farther away from wariness.

Now she was really cold. She rose from the bench and entered the house. By feel, she moved into darkness. Her groping hand found and turned the knob of an interior door. Behind that door, stairs led downward. With a practiced move, she took two steps down, closed the door behind her, and flicked a light switch.

In the large basement she entered, she could finally relax. A big table filled its center, most of its surface cluttered with computers and their peripherals. Industrial shelves with manuals, printouts, and additional hardware ran along one wall. A good quality couch, the newest item in the room, sat beneath blacked-out basement windows. A hot water heater and a furnace took up one corner, and a small cooking area huddled in another. The other spaces were behind two closed doors: a small bathroom with a shower, and a former storage room barely large enough for a double bed.

Key dumped her knapsack and got ready for bed. But finding sleep wasn't easy. Her dad's death intruded again, and the new jolt of seeing Crash Davies at the bar immediately made it worse. She'd caught sight of Crash through the pass-through opening from the bar's small kitchen. It seemed unlikely he had noticed her. But had he? What did she really know about him? Enough to trust him any more than anyone else?

There was no answer to that last question, even though she kept scratching it like a scab until the thoughts she'd had out in the woods returned. Crash was just an old detail. The real issue was whether her Seattle string had run out, as everything inevitably did. Tomorrow she'd think about running again.

Exhaustion finally let sleep in.

❀ ❀ ❀

Crash Davies adjusted the sleeping bag so his shoulders were covered. In the dark early morning, he luxuriated in a state of drowsiness. As wakefulness slowly took hold, he assessed his situation, including what it might mean that he'd seen Key Flanerty at his gig last night.

The gig itself was nothing special. The drummer and lead guitar were on time, but since he and his bass guitar were playing with the D-Crabs for the first time, it took a while before the trio got in sync.

The crowd had been typical, too—laid-back Seattle, casual in dress and expectation. He'd seen many of the same people at the wine- or beer-themed bistros scattered over Capitol Hill, in Belltown and, more recently, at venues farther south. They were light years removed from the high-octane techies who frequented other types of places, especially in Bellevue—or, as he called it, Microsoftville. He liked to think that the spirit of Grunge still lived in the souls of the people he played for. For sure, he wasn't any Kurt Cobain, but Kurt's crowd, like the one tonight, probably lived with the same simple rule: When the music started, it started, and it ended when it ended. No other explanation was necessary.

That was the attitude he'd eventually adopted for everything: Take life as it comes. Do what you think is interesting, instead of what other people tell you to do. He'd tried that standard outwardly-driven path and finally decided it wasn't for him. Just wait for the next gig—musical or something else—and get what you can from what comes along. That way you can follow your curiosity when it calls.

Even though he'd been at it for a couple of years, he was still experimenting with that lifestyle. He'd come to think of it as changing from a guided missile into a butterfly. Weird comparison, he knew. An

English teacher would probably red-pencil it, but it felt accurate. His parents had been too involved in their own work to give him much direction. They did buy him opportunities: education, summer trips, internships. As a teenager, he began to wonder if he'd missed something. After three years in two colleges, he decided that that question was worth answering, and he'd been wandering ever since.

Life became a string of short-lived samplings. He had little trouble finding part-time jobs, like his present one as a janitor in an art glass studio. He had technical skills that always surprised his employers, and they often tried to keep him on the payroll. But his curiosity had a time limit, and he moved on. The only constant was music. He liked the loose structure of the musical community, the chance to observe oddball patrons, and the music itself. If the gig was a bad one, he could simply decide not to play with that band again. There were always other bands, and never enough bass players.

Along the way, he'd met a few interesting people. He liked the glass artist he worked for now. Earlier, when he had a job installing audio systems, he'd met some of the new high-tech millionaires. They were a mixed bag in person, some accessible, others withdrawn, and a few insufferably entitled.

One job was particularly memorable. He'd installed a really good sound system in a modest home in north Seattle. The owner was a former football player, though he hadn't identified himself that way. Crash put together pictures he'd seen in *The Seattle Times* and on TV with the lithe, dark-haired client who towered over him, and the name on the contract clicked: Gary Seasons.

He might be recalling that particular job because of the news piece he'd watched yesterday. Seasons had just been named to a new position with some environmental agency. And another stray fact returned: Seasons' cell number. After the area code, the numbers were the same as Crash's birthday, 4/08/1991.

This brief focus on Seasons disappeared quickly. Seeing Key was another matter entirely. The image of her last night was embedded in his brain. He wasn't sure why. Knowing her and having her disappear so abruptly was the one exception in an otherwise satisfying pattern of

14

acquaintances and departures. Key had fascinated him when they met. Her looks and expressions. Even the way she kept blowing him off. He'd watched her in the student boarding house until she left after only a month. Then she was gone, and a hole in the smooth fabric of his existence appeared. He didn't exactly miss her, but he wondered frequently about her constant air of watchfulness that sometimes looked like fear.

It had to be her he saw at the pass-through behind the bar. He wasn't sure until he caught the familiar watchful expression. During the rest of the gig, he kept looking for her, trying to pretend he wasn't doing so. His subterfuge must have succeeded, because the Key he knew would have dropped everything and left if she'd found anyone crowding her.

He felt torn. Should he let things be? Finally drop his curiosity about Key? Or try to renew a connection with her?

Later he'd think more about that. Meanwhile, his memory returned to her small face and worried eyes one more time before he dozed off again.

NOVEMBER 2

Laura Dickens awoke with a mental image of bearded Professor Williams. She hadn't thought of him in years. Why now? She knew the answer.

Williams had been her advisor, an academic who didn't fit the mold of his colleagues. Their world was one of statistical studies and the science of forestry. Williams knew the academic sources, but he also knew the industry from early years as a logger. She imagined his voice now.

"You want my advice, choose any ecological field except logging to build your career around. Logging's a sump hole, with a gravitational pull of its own. If it were only trees, you'd be fine. But it isn't. It's big business, with practices you don't want to know about. It's also a tough business. Loggers don't like outsiders, and they like to settle things physically, out of sight, in the woods."

He thought a bit more and offered final advice.

"Some other field of study will make your life easier."

So what had she done? Ended up with a job that would put her right in the middle of a hot logging controversy at Isadka Valley. But no matter. It was just one more challenge, and she fed on challenges—especially physical ones. She'd said exactly that to Professor Williams, and he'd looked at her with a knowing smile, half skepticism and half pity. Good to be reminded of his admonition, but why should this situation be any different from the many others she'd met and mastered?

On the farm where she grew up, she chose the chores that were the hardest, that would immerse her in the challenge of completing, or, better yet, mastering. At the University she found rowing, a sport she'd never tried before but excelled at as if born to it. It was ordered and demanding, and came with the ultimate ending point: pure physical exhaustion. Then you started over.

True, she was about to enter the second half of her twenties with not much heft to her resume and only a small savings account, the remainder of what her parents left her when they died. She had a college degree in forestry and an MBA. She'd found no promising jobs in the forestry sector—it was actually shedding jobs as it introduced new technologies and restructured ownership. The MBA she'd added as in-

19

surance was useless in a recession. When her mother got sick, and she had to go back east of the Cascades to care for her, the only work she found was with an outdoor recreation company that itself was having trouble. So she abandoned the east side.

Luckily, back on the west side, in Seattle, she found a temporary job at the State Department of Natural Resources. And she found this apartment—if you could call it that. Small living quarters like these began to exist in Seattle about the time she finished at the University. Now, they were concrete and glass weeds sprouting all over the city. If she rose from where she sat on a convertible couch and took four steps past a coffee table and one upholstered chair, she could put her hand on the front door. Add a tiny kitchen area and a sleeping loft, and she had, in 400 square feet, everything she needed. But not what she craved: empty walls where she could hang outdoor equipment.

That thought brought her up short. Face it—you don't need day dreams. You need to get to work. Use the cramped apartment as motivation to get something better. Whether or not the new job seems challenging enough, just do it.

She stood and looked over the tops of the shorter buildings in the surrounding cityscape. The tips of the Cascades rose above their roof-line, and she fixed her sight on an approximate point where the interstate crossed Snoqualmie Pass, going toward the east side of the state. Less than fifty miles beyond that stood the house where she and her family had lived. Life there felt more fulfilling, a simple existence that generated its own sense of purpose. Rowing had its satisfactions, but it was never a purpose—and once you won a race or ended a season, that was it. Her last season had ended five years ago. Since then, she'd never paused, and therefore not yet discovered why she was working so hard or for what.

It dawned on her that it wasn't the apartment or the technical nature of new and unfamiliar duties that fueled her unease. She knew she'd plow ahead, regardless. But she needed to give more attention to what she wanted in the long run.

Today's office work would be no help in that regard, just more paper pushing. But tomorrow sounded interesting. Because a colleague

20

was sick, she would make a field visit to the Isadka Valley site. She was well aware that logging was coming under greater scrutiny for its environmental impacts. And newer concerns about population spread and logging practices were growing, especially about how those practices impacted people's safety.

The Isadka Valley project could be a real chance to get an oar in. She'd give it her all and deal with obstacles as they came up. Energy and determination would win out. Thanks for the dream reminder, Professor Williams, but I can handle this. And maybe I'll discover what that dream was about, or dream something else.

With that mindset, she headed to work.

As Gary Seasons walked into the Seattle Seahawks' training facility on Lake Washington, he couldn't take his mind off the email that had popped up this morning. He hadn't wanted to open it. It might bring back memories of the days when he lived an isolated existence with his mother and his brothers and sisters. When he lived a life just barely above subsistence level. A time he would rather forget. But he had to see what the email said.

On the surface, the request was straightforward.

Been a while. How about a visit? Free any afternoon next week. No agenda. Be good for us to get together. Let me know. Curt

He'd had stared at the screen, trying to read what was behind the words. Nothing from Curt Longcart was ever straightforward. Any truth was always a mixture of what you saw or heard and what you wished you hadn't.

For a moment, he wondered if Curt's email could have anything to do with a project at Isadka Valley he was assessing as part of his new job. Out of curiosity, he had looked up the origin of the name. Turned out "Isadka" meant "family haven" in the Lushootseed language, so it might have been a settlement near where his own forebears lived.

Curt once had a minor interest in logging projects but supposedly had gotten out of them. What if he hadn't? And why would he be concerned about the new assignment of his former employee, anyway?

21

An enthusiastic voice pulled Gary away from that line of thought. "Hey Chief Hawk, how's it goin'?"

Gary glanced over and recognized the man as one of several people who often clustered near the entrance to the Seahawks' training area. Fans congregated at any Seahawks event, togged out in team gear, trying to get the attention of their favorites.

Gary waved at the fan. He owed him that much. It was three years since he'd worn a player's jersey, but here was a guy remembering him. He was also a guy who, along with thousands of others, had earned Gary a lot of money.

Chief Hawk. He used to hear that nickname often, now seldom. Some reporter had coined it, and it stuck. Not all that imaginative, but it was popular. Never mind that he'd grown up some distance south of his tribal home on the Skagit River. Or that his nearly full-blooded Mountain Salish father had disappeared early, and that his part-Indian mother was vague about her origins. Tribal heritage wasn't big at home. But to the Seattle locals, he was an "Indian kid" who, as he advanced in football, became "that local Indian phenom" and eventually "Chief Hawk."

Today he was at the training facility, along with other ex-players, to remember a former teammate who had been killed by a drunk driver. Gary had been closer to Ernie than most of the others had, finding an unexpected connection with a teetotaling devout Georgia cracker. They lost contact after Gary left the Hawks, and Ernie wore the jersey for another two years. But he felt he owed Ernie his presence at a team meeting to honor him today. Naturally, the coach used the occasion, and Ernie's name, to fire up desire for another championship. But at least he did it tastefully.

Gary left as soon as he could and drove up I-405 and across Lake Washington on I-90. Shutting out the partial view of downtown Seattle that peaked above the residential ridge in front of him, he reflected on the contrast between life on the field and off the field. Then, every detail of his life had been attended to by someone else. Today it was all up to him to succeed in a new job. No coach, no playbook—only expectations that, with little guidance, he'd figure out what needed to be done.

He reached an established building just north of Pioneer Square and took an elevator to the sixth floor. The sign on the door looked freshly painted and read "O.P.U.S.: ONE PUGET SOUND" with "The Puget Sound Commission" in smaller letters below. Inside, one large room held a conference table with seats for sixteen. Beyond it, a door was open to a small office with two desks. One was his, the other was for a secretary to be named later.

He had a small pile of documents to review. Nothing important yet. Most likely a test that someone designed to see what kind of output he was capable of. That pile would grow a lot larger as the commission got down to work.

He straightened, swiveled his chair, and took in the downward view across rooftops to the Sound. A ferry was docking, a sight repeated every hour on the hour, except early and late in the day when the turnaround was faster. Less frequently, he caught sight of the Sounder commuter train as it left downtown Seattle for its trip on to Tacoma. Beyond was the northern tip of West Seattle and, in the distance, Kitsap Peninsula and the Olympic Mountains.

The view was a pleasure, but no real escape from the words on his computer screen. That early morning message from Curt Longcart crowded his consciousness again.

It had been more than ten years since he worked regularly at Longcart Motors. That is, if sitting around in the showroom could be called work. All Curt really wanted was a customer magnet, and he got that with the name recognition provided by an Indian high school football star. Gary winced at the memory of the awkward conversations he was expected to have with strangers. That awkward feeling had never disappeared, though he memorized the act. After a while, pretending interest and repeating the same words over and over got to be something he could do without noticing. He only had to haul out the old act when he did PR for the Seahawks.

When he was cut from the Hawks, Curt stopped calling so much. Sure, he'd invite Gary to ceremonial openings, and Curt still occasionally used old pictures of him in TV spots, but there were no more references to "my good friend Gary." During his last visit, Gary saw that most of the football memorabilia celebrating his career was no longer on display.

So why a meeting now? Could it have anything to do with those other conversations years ago, the ones they kept quiet? Curt had given financial support to Gary's family. To the extent that this assistance was public at all, it was tied to Gary's "job." But the real money—much more than his reported salary from Curt—went directly to a bank account in Gary's mother's name. Had the true numbers been known—the unreported deposits, the hundred dollar bills passed with a handshake, the free servicing of a "loaner" car, the clothes delivered without a return address—they would have been subject to investigations by high school sports associations and, later, by the NCAA.

Curt never used the gifts as leverage, not overtly. After Gary made it with the pros, he began to forget that heavy weight hanging over his head. Now he wondered if it hadn't been there all along.

No matter how he looked at it, he came to the same conclusion: His best bet was to call Curt and get past whatever it was he wanted. There was no other way to find out what was really going on.

Tomorrow he'd call the private number he still remembered.

NOVEMBER 3

Laura was used to early mornings. Five years of rowing a boat at dawn, regardless of the weather, had conditioned her body to crave that kind of start to the day. Given the chance, she still counted on the energy of first light to take a bite out of the toughest problems facing her.

In recent weeks, the morning regimen had another benefit: It got her out of her apartment. Today the bonus was not a lake, but instead the wet ribbon of I-5 North. She should get to Mount Vernon in about half the time it would take during rush hour. A light drizzle that was trying to become rain hardly slowed her.

Trouble was, shortening the drive wouldn't straighten the pretzel of job issues she needed to sort out. Maybe a torus was a better image than a pretzel. But both figures, the math one and the homey one, were basically the same. No matter where you started tracing them, you'd end up back where you started.

As she drove, she recalled a surprise encounter yesterday. One of the veterans in the office–Herb Katz–invited her to have coffee together. She'd wondered what the pudgy, somewhat disheveled older man in the cubicle opposite hers wanted to talk about. He explained in his first sentence

"It seems to me you either don't like what you're doing, or possibly don't get how you fit into what goes on around here."

He was right, but his presumption made her bristle.

"What gives you that idea?"

"Pretty easy. You're not the first newcomer I've seen with those problems. I had them myself. You get up and walk around pretty often. And there's that look on your face, a cross between boredom and irritation. You cover up that last mood okay, but it's there."

Strangely, those words calmed her. At least, here was someone she could talk to.

"You look as if you've been around here a while."

He nodded.

"This office, going on five years. State government jobs for more than twenty."

"And you don't get irritated with the wheel spinning, or with examining the same issues over and over again?"

"Sure I do. Thought of quitting. But then I realized that we do play a helpful role."

"Which is?"

"Taking difficult issues away from the political infighting for a while. You know, a time-out or a cooling-off period. Major issues usually don't get solved in one pass, and sometimes not even in three or four. Things take time. We run simulations, refine ideas. Our work is often the catalyst for agreement that wins out over political dueling."

That made some sense. As long as they were talking, she might as well make use of the man's perspective.

"How about Isadka? I keep going over the same figures, sometimes in probability models, maps, cost benefit tables. They don't change, but I'm supposed to find something new by going over and over them again?"

Katz sighed through a sheepish grin.

"I was talking ideal situation. You're right; it's often hard to see the forest through the trees—no pun intended. There are lulls, sometimes long ones, in our forward progress. Our system's imperfect—what else can I say—except maybe to quote Churchill that democracy's the worst form of government except for any other that's been tried."

Laura rewarded him with a smile, but kept going.

"So Isadka sits there until the final verdict's in on Gideon, and we keep reading the same reports?"

A logging project across the river from houses in Gideon—a small town in the Cascade foothills—had been completed almost two decades ago. The project was a collection of small parcels at the top of a steep slope facing the housing site, and it went ahead under permissive regulations that pertained only to small parcels. A small parcel could be logged closer to the hillside's edge than larger parcels were allowed to be. If a big operation could bundle small parcels together into a large parcel, but still keep the small parcel exemptions, more lumber could be logged near the steep slopes. But the hillside might also become more fragile and dangerous. Bottom line: a lot more money could be made at some potential human cost.

Four years ago, the worst case had happened. Unusually heavy rains weakened the hillside. A large chunk of it gave way in the middle of the night, and more than 150 people were buried in a massive mudslide. Most media placed blame for the deadly slide squarely on the forestry company, and the press had a field day linking big-business forestry practices and death in one story, well before any investigation was complete.

In the aftermath of Gideon, the issue of small logging parcels and their regulation got a lot of scrutiny. The investigation so far was inconclusive: Unsafe logging might have contributed to the slide, but scientists could not say so for sure. In the long term, geologic change caused slides in the Gideon area every 150 years, anyway. A coalition of owners with smaller holdings, plus Indian tribes, had asked for continued leniency when it came to small parcels of land.

Katz swirled the liquid at the bottom of his cup, took a sip, then looked at her.

"Isadka's a perfect example. Like all logging projects, it involves jobs as well as preservation, profits and risk. We need to encourage forward progress there, without taking sides, even before the full verdict is in on Gideon. Otherwise, we'll be looking at a very public fight between the environmentalists and the big enterprises that own Isadka. So yes, you can look forward to boring days reviewing old reports; but you might also come up with information that will break the logjam."

He pretended a wince, and grinned.

"Sorry, I can't help myself."

Laura had begun to like Katz. Maybe someday she'd be able to see things the way he did. But not yet.

Something else got in the way, too. She'd begun to realize that she wanted something tangible and human in her work. She hadn't found that yet. A job at Natural Resources wasn't like rowing, where at least you knew the weather. In the meantime, how could she compensate? One answer would be to do nothing. But she didn't want that. She'd keep on moving forward until she felt pushback.

The highway past Everett was almost free of traffic, and she sped up.

❉ ❉ ❉

The big man wore a suit today, fitted well enough so the first thing you saw wasn't his growing paunch. Time had added wrinkles to his broad face and made a prominent nose look even bigger.

Gary took Curt Longcart's extended hand and returned a firm grasp.

"Gary, Gary. God, it's been a while. Where've you been keeping yourself, stranger?"

The eyes gleamed, a display without warmth.

"Just gettin' the work done. Like football, only a different job. You know. Keeping at it and getting ready for the big one."

Not much like football at all, actually. But then he remembered their old verbal drill.

Curt upped the wattage of his smile. It fit well with the bright lights and the array of gleaming vehicles around them, though in the moment it only made Gary's wariness stronger.

"Haven't changed at all. You always got it up for the big ones, and you delivered. C'mon."

Curt spun around, making a follow-me gesture over his shoulder. Gary walked after him through a door off to one side of the show-room. The interior of the dealership hadn't changed at all. The same old steel chairs and plastic-topped conference table were dingy part-ners to the glitz of the showroom. The place was perfect Curt: money for show next door, and stingy disregard for the people doing the real work.

They sat facing each other across the scarred gray surface. While Curt called for coffee, Gary examined his old boss.

There were hints of gray in his full black hair, but up close you could see it had been professionally dyed. His trademark ponytail was shorter. Despite the vigorous façade, it was clear how hard he was working to look younger than his late sixties.

Coffee arrived. Curt waited until the door closed behind the young lady who brought it. Then he looked at Gary with eyes that darkened to a steady stare.

"Let's get down to business. I hear you got work in Olympia as an assistant with someone in the legislature."

"Yeah. For a few months now."

Gary waited while an expression he was all too familiar with settled on Curt's face.

"Gary, I want you to do something for me."

Immediately Curt shook his head like a dog shedding water and flashed the sincere look again.

"No. No. That came out wrong. I'm sorry, kid. The recession put me under a lot of pressure. Doing better now, but you still gotta be careful."

Gary had seen that act many times: personality on demand. The quick-change artist switching his costume. At one time he'd been around to help with those changes and knew just how much Curt's motives stayed the same, regardless of the disguise.

But there was something else Gary knew: how to keep his own feelings hidden. You can't grow up Indian and not know that. He made an effort to be bland and affable in return.

"Hey, Curt. No worries. You've always had my back, and there's no way I can forget all the things you've done to help my family."

Curt nodded slowly and settled into the middle ground between handler and benefactor.

"Now, about this new job."

"Yeah. How'd you know?"

Curt grinned.

"You may have left, but I keep tabs on how you're doing. I care, you know."

Gary allowed a guarded smile.

"Nice to know that."

They were silent while Gary waited for the other man to show his hand. Curt glanced around quickly, as if something stood between

31

them and the bare walls. Ready, he clasped his meaty hands and leaned forward.

"So, how's it going?"

"Still learning the ropes."

"You're at One Puget Sound, what they're calling OPUS, the governor's new advisory group, right? Tell me about it."

"I staff a group that's trying to encourage state agencies, businesses, and tribes to work together on the future of Puget Sound. You know, get the major players that have a stake in the Sound to protect it as a common asset."

"So how about you, how you doing financially?"

Uh-oh, here we go. The question about OPUS was only a lead-in. Now the real stuff starts.

"Okay."

"Your family, too?"

Gary tried to keep his voice even.

"Do you mind if I ask where this is going, Curt?"

"Not at all."

No change in his tone, but Curt's gaze turned darker. He sat back, holding his eyes steady.

"Could be, though, that if you need more money, it could be arranged."

There it was.

"In exchange for what?"

Gary sat back, too. What remained of the friendship charade disappeared with that added distance. Curt's old voice took over—the voice that only gave orders.

"Let's review a little. Seems to me I remember an Indian kid who needed a lot of help and got it. So did his family. Most people would stay grateful for that."

"And I am, Curt. Always will be. But what's that got to do with what we're talking about?"

A crafty look flashed across Curt's face.

"Okay, then here's the deal. You know I've got financial interests that go beyond cars. I built a couple of strip malls that did well for a while. Not so much now. Same with real estate. I've also picked up logging options on promising sites for when logging comes back stronger. That's starting to happen, but the slide at Gideon didn't help."

What an understatement. The Gideon slide had buried people and homes.

They could sidestep a straight conversation all morning.

"I get it. What do you really want?"

"I think you know already. I want eyes and ears on the ground so there'll be no surprises. That's you. And if you don't think so, I still have a few stories to tell from the past."

"Old news. No one's interested anymore."

"Maybe. But your mom might find life is harder. Little inconveniences add up fast. She wouldn't have any idea why they're happening."

A red haze blurred Gary's eyes and he gripped the table edge. Through that veil of anger, he imagined shoving the heavy table over onto Curt, seeing him fall to the floor with the table's weight pinning him down. He could make that happen almost as easily as he could stand up. It would be such a great feeling. Relief and revenge wrapped into one.

But he waited for a practiced surge of icy reality to drench the flames. He had made similar calculations over the years. What would he gain? Nothing. What would he lose? A lot. Curt was disliked for all kinds of reasons, but deranged ex-football players, their brains scrambled in too many Sunday face-offs, had become a tabloid fixture. He knew he was vulnerable.

Another thought scratched at his consciousness. The Curt he knew would not apply pressure so openly, wouldn't threaten punishment if he didn't cooperate. Curt had always been heavy on appearing affable while he held his cards close.

So why the change now? A quick answer occurred: Maybe Curt himself was unusually vulnerable. To whom? Maybe to someone more powerful than he was. A real Mr. Big lurking behind the big guy. If that was true, then he might get leverage of his own if he found out what was really going on.

He forced his hands to relax, and returned them to his lap. His best option was to play along.

"Tell me more."

NOVEMBER 5

"Hi Walt, and Happy Birthday."

Walt Vickers, slouched in a wheelchair, smiled pleasantly as he accepted a small box of his favorite Frango mints. Key couldn't remember a time when he wasn't smiling. How was that possible? Especially here.

She hated the smell of the place. Smells had always been the sense that registered first and strongest for her. This one was old age: body odors, medicines, disinfectants, and an all-purpose floral scent, chosen, she supposed, to mask the other smells and ending up being the worst of them.

Alki View was accurately named for its location. Its main lounge and a narrow deck attached to its long side came with a broad view that looked across Puget Sound to the residential hills of Queen Anne and Magnolia. At one edge you saw a slice of downtown Seattle and, at the other, the northern tip of the Olympic Mountains. From the deck you could see Alki Beach below.

An ideal place to spend your last years, you might think, and Key had thought so when she first set eyes on the place from the outside, focusing only on the view. Then she learned about the inside, with its routines, limited programs, isolated rooms, and smells. From then on she hated Walt's surroundings and, even more, the thought that she might someday be one of its listless inhabitants, warehoused like strays at the pound.

But Walt Vickers was here. He said he looked forward to her visits. The best part of any day, he'd repeated often. That was enough to keep her coming back. He owned the house where she lived in the basement. A spontaneous humane gesture on his part had changed her life and led to a relationship that surprised both of them.

She'd been seventeen, a runaway, new to Seattle and clueless about how to survive in a big city. She found a sublet in a student boarding house near the U. But the expense, plus close proximity to others—particularly Crash—made her want to move. For a few weeks she stayed at a hostel. But then the unseasonably warm weather gave way to rain and temperatures that dipped into the twenties, just as her mea-

37

ger cash ran out. She was forced outside on a night when the flu caught her. She still had no idea how she ended up under a tree in the woods near Walt's house, wracked with a cough and burning with fever. He found her and took her in.

There was a quizzical look on his face.

"What?"

"You mean, what am I thinking? Well, at the moment that you're still the tough little thing I found four years ago. Look a lot better, though. Got more meat on you. Why do you look so worried?"

If that question had come from anyone else Key would have blown it off. But this was a person she came close to trusting. Not all the way, of course. Only her father had earned that.

"I get the feeling I'm being followed."

"Proof?"

"Nothing definite."

"Do you really think someone still wants that tape?"

"Gotta assume yes."

Walt rolled himself back a couple of feet, sat thinking, then rolled back to where he had been.

"The tape's still hidden and safe?"

"No reason why not. I haven't checked."

"Probably best not to. If someone's really watching you, that could lead them to it. Anyway, they'd about have to tear down the whole house to find it, and you'd sure know about that."

Silence filled the space between them, and Key became aware of nurses' voices, footsteps, doors closing. Walt cleared his throat.

"Speaking of the house, there's something I need to talk to you about."

His tone was different. If she had a choice, she'd leave without hearing the rest. Walt looked right at her.

"Got some news today. No surprise."

She guessed what was coming. She'd known it since Walt began passing out and had to move from his house to this place.

"I've got about three months more. If that."

She allowed herself to open the freezer door, the sub-zero place inside where she waited out bad things. She'd found that place as a little girl, and knew how to stay there as long as it took until she felt safe enough to edge out of it. The peacefulness of the past few years had been an illusion. She saw the future. Wait out time in the freezer. Get out. Run again.

For the moment, she nodded and waited. No other emotion. He wouldn't expect it. Walt allowed a small smile, as if he'd already figured that out. His words sped up.

"I spent part of yesterday with my lawyer. Then I talked to Jim Purgis—you know, my friend at AlkiSteel. I simplified my will. You get everything, house and land. And the money in my accounts after liabilities are paid off. Purgis says he can keep the maintenance arrangement with the mill going as long as he's around. At that point, you can…"

"I don't want it!"

She hadn't meant to raise her voice, but panic can do that to you. She'd been ready for a lot of things, just not this.

Walt's smile just got bigger.

"Right on schedule, just like I expected. This time you don't get off so easy."

"Easy? More like you're punishing me with a favor I don't want."

"You don't have to tell me that. You made it clear from the beginning that you want no baggage, no strings. Nothing that would force you out of your gypsy existence. But I'm giving you everything so you have to make a choice."

"I make my own choices, and I'm not about to change the ones I've made."

The expression on his face reminded her that he was no stranger to firm decisions.

"Well, looks as if you'll have to deal with my choices, too. That's actually a good thing. We've talked about that before."

"Yeah, we did, and am I saying anything different?"

"No you aren't."

They sat in silence. Key calmed enough to register how the focus had shifted to her. Hey, she wasn't the one dying. She spoke before that flash turned into anything else, like wanting to cry. That goddamn urge always complicated things.

"Anyway, sorry about your news."

He waved a hand listlessly.

"Don't bother yourself, and don't worry, either. It was going to happen. Now I know. Let the doctors worry about the details. The only details I need to think about are disposing of my property."

She couldn't think of anything else to say. He rescued her.

"Go on, get out of here and do what you got to do. Let me know if someone is really after you. Not sure exactly what I can do about it, but I've got a few resources."

She got up and almost started toward the door. Except for the first night when Walt rescued her, they had never touched, much less hugged. Now her hand had a will of its own as it reached out and settled on Walt's shoulder.

He looked up at her for a moment, his eyes moist. Then he turned away without speaking. She hesitated a moment longer, seeking the words hiding just behind her lips.

She knew they were there, but she couldn't speak them. She left.

❋ ❋ ❋

The car windows kept fogging up, and despite a down jacket, Crash could feel a chill crawling up his backbone. His reasoning was beginning to feel foggy, too.

Okay, he wanted to see Key again. Just why was still not clear. Because he was curious about what she'd become and how she ended up working in the kitchen of a bar? Or because he liked her? The decision to try to meet her after work had seemed clear enough a few hours ago without such introspection.

His guess had been right: She did work regularly at the same bar. Waiting until the evening crowd was large enough, he had slipped in the front door and, with a clutch of drinkers between him and the bar, hung out until Key's face appeared at the pass-through window to the kitchen.

He had left right away and driven aimlessly for an hour to waste time. As closing time approached at 1 am, he parked across the street from the bar and waited.

After another half hour Key came out, a backpack slung from one shoulder, and started walking down Admiral Boulevard. He couldn't miss her tiny size and spiked black hair. Less definable, but also part of her identity, was the way she sought out the closeness of buildings and trees, as if she were constantly on the lookout for a hiding place.

Her destination was a parked car a block away. With a 5 pm start time at the bar, she apparently found street parking before commuters returned home and took all the curbside spaces. Headlights out, Crash followed her, driving slowly. He was careful to stay back. She got into a car. He waited until her lights went on and she pulled out into the street.

When her car turned the corner, he made a quick assessment: What more would he learn by following her? If she spotted him, she might think he was stalking her. Maybe better to call it a night, to think of a different approach.

He hesitated until he saw a dark motorcycle appear at the intersection ahead, its headlight off. It turned in the direction Key had taken.

Now Crash was immediately on alert. Why would a motorcycle's headlight be off at night, unless someone was trying not to be seen? It could just be one of the late-leaving patrons from the bar, trying to avoid a DUI. Or someone could be following Key. His gut told him to allow for the worst.

Crash pulled away from the curb and turned at the intersection. He held back, following Key from a distance as she drove down Admiral and took the exit for Avalon, before Admiral merged with the bridge to I-5. At each turn, the motorcycle stayed steady behind her. It slowed as Key turned left into the parking lot for the AlkiSteel mill. Crash saw, or imagined, hesitation on the motorcyclist's part. The biker had ample space to get by Key and accelerate the moment she began her turn. Instead he slowed almost to a stop at the driveway before gunning his engine. The sound of a deep rumble receded as the motorcycle climbed the steeply-rising street at high speed.

Crash doused his lights and waited on idle as he watched Key's car cross the AlkiSteel parking lot. With headlights still out, he turned into the lot, driving far enough to see Key's car veer right and disappear into a wooded area along its side.

He parked by the side of the mill. Grabbing a flashlight from the glove compartment, he walked thirty yards or so along the woods, guided by exterior lights from the mill and a half-moon above. It was easy to spot a gravel driveway leading into the trees. Moving carefully, with his light off, he groped a short distance until he sensed a barrier ahead. A quick flash of the light revealed a free-standing garage. Working his way around it, he flicked the light on again and spotted a narrow trail that disappeared into the trees. He could not go any farther without light, so he masked the beam with splayed fingers and moved forward.

The trail snaked around larger trees. Soon he found himself in a clearing that held a much larger structure. Shades or curtains covered its windows, but he could see dim light around the edges of the window closest to a flight of entry stairs.

Decision time. Key might not answer the door, and she'd be angry if she did. But a sense that she was in danger had brought him this far.

Do it.

❋ ❋ ❋

Key stood stock still in the entry hall. A ceiling fixture with a low-watt bulb lit the narrow space, harshly revealing how lonely and disused it had become. Her finger was on the switch when she heard a noise outside. It had no particular character, except to disturb the early-morning stillness.

She turned off the light and strained to listen. Nothing. Just like the other night. She was on edge. She didn't believe in all that sixth sense crap, but she kept imagining something was there.

Had she locked the front door? It was second nature, but better check. Her hand was on the knob when she heard another sound. This time she knew she wasn't imagining; it was a voice.

She didn't move, straining to hear. There it was again.

"Key. It's me. Crash. I know you're there. It's important."

She stayed silent. The voice on the other side continued, rising in volume. A sharp rap on the door punctuated the words.

Crash! She wanted nothing to do with that pesky jerk. But she also didn't want him to attract anyone else. Crash was a bother, but at least she knew who he was. Talking to him posed a smaller danger than the noise he was making.

And how had he found her house? Did that mean others might know, too? If this hideout was compromised, she'd have to get out. Right away.

She opened the door a crack. The size and shape were right, but in near darkness she could only see blurry features. His head was just above hers. That fit. Not enough light to spot his most unmistakable marker—red-orange hair, never parted, cascading down both sides and the back of his head.

It was, finally, the posture that convinced her. Crash was the only person she knew who stood in a hunched-forward semi-slouch. It was so bothersome to her that, when they lived in the same house, she avoided him just because she didn't want to see him standing like that.

She didn't trust him. On the other hand, he'd never done anything to make her distrust him, if she could ignore the irritation he caused. Main thing: he already knew where she lived. Why not find out what else he knew?

She opened the door halfway and he entered. Then she locked it, turned on the flashlight, and led him down to the basement.

Crash blinked hard. If the house gave an impression of dereliction from the outside, even a quick glance at the interior said the opposite. The basement wasn't neat, but systems had been carefully tended.

A battery of new LEDs and old fluorescents bathed a large basement space in an instant glare. As he looked down and away, he noticed first a flexible cable running along a side wall. One end exited beside the vent pipe of a relatively new gas furnace. The other end led to an even newer fan assembly that emitted a low hum. Crash raised his eyes and took in two walls with evenly-spaced windows, all of which were painted black.

Key stood beside a long table full of electronic equipment, her arms crossed and an angry look on her face. Behind her, he noticed a kitchen area and a door beside it through which a washbasin was visible. Best to break the ice gently.

"Quite a place you have here."

"Cut the crap. How'd you find it?"

"I saw you the other evening and wanted to find out how you were doing, so I... decided to follow you home."

He was immediately aware how bad that sounded.

Her retort came out swinging.

"As if I believe that."

He held up his hands and tried to explain.

"Look, I'd actually decided not to follow you. But when you got in your car, some guy on a motorcycle started after you and he didn't have his headlight on. I hung back, watched him all the way to the mill, then went after you on the trail. I just wanted to give you a heads up. It's cool."

That made her even angrier.

"Who have you told about this place?"

"No one. How could I? Until a few minutes ago I didn't even know it existed."

"The motorcycle, if there was one, could have followed you to the club."

That didn't exactly make sense. A thought immediately flashed: She's more afraid than she wants to let on.

"Why should anyone want to follow me? Or you?"

She looked away and threw her arms up.

"What do you want before I tell you to get out?"

That hurt some, but he was still curious.

"Want? Just to know you're safe and maybe to know what you've been doing. I don't like to lose track of friends. Don't have many of them."

"I'm a friend? Just because we lived in the same house for two months, four years ago? Maybe you don't know how little that meant to me."

She put real heat behind her words. Funny, that made him more relaxed. She was beginning to be again the girl he remembered.

"Well, I haven't forgotten."

In the pause that followed, Crash went on quickly.

"Judging by the cabling there on the wall, you're getting your utilities from somewhere other than the city. So someone must know you're here. Why are you so afraid of my knowing?"

Key's face conveyed her answer: no way, Jose. She rose, walked a few paces away, and turned back, her arms crossed.

"You said you wanted to know what I've done in the last four years. Nothing. I worked odd jobs, and now I'm cook at a bar that can only afford unknown music. There. You can leave."

He pointed at her worktable.

"So what's all that equipment for? Just so you can look around the net? That's an impressive setup."

Her glare bristled.

"Hardly. I blog."

Immediately she looked away, as if regretting what she had revealed.

"You do? That's great. About what, and where?"

"None of your business. Is that why you're here? So you can let a bunch of sorry fuckers know my identity?"

The force behind her words was a blast of frigid air.

"No, damn it, no! How could I? I just found out you blogged just a few seconds ago."

"So you say. All I know for sure is that you followed me and know where I live. If you try to do anything with that information, you'll be the one regretting."

Man, was she trying to look threatening. Her almost-black eyes were like diamond-tipped drills. Her little fists were tightly balled by her side. Ragged black bangs and baggy clothing hid almost all the rest of her. On a larger person all that might have seemed dangerous. On her it was fascinating.

45

He shrugged, saw a pad on the edge of the big table, and took two steps to pick it up, along with a nearby pen. He couldn't help glancing at scattered print-outs. One was from a website he recognized. On another, he saw what might be part of a URL, "mittandhiss". He scribbled his name and contact information on the pad and handed it to Key. As he did so, he repeated to himself the strange partial address he'd just seen: Mittandhiss. He'd check it later.

"My email and cell in case you want to reach me."

She didn't even look at the writing before tossing the pad back onto the table. It landed face down. She half turned away from him and crossed her arms.

He started up the stairs, realizing how little he knew about Key. Where had she gotten this house? How could such a derelict place have electricity and all that equipment? Why was she so supersensitive about being a blogger?

Those were details. Main outcome: He'd made contact and talked to her. He knew more now than he had before. But he still had no idea why she seemed so afraid.

NOVEMBER 7

L aura saw a rangy figure approaching. Finally, they were getting their schedules straight. A ride out here two days ago hadn't been so successful. She'd walked around the Isadka Valley site; but without the foreman to answer questions, that two-hour trip had been pretty much a waste of time.

She took Rick Groff's extended hand. They'd met once before in the office when he had come to Seattle. He'd shown her pictures of his family, so she knew that he had two teenage kids with curly hair like his. Otherwise, he was an outdoorsman in his thirties, in a woolen long-sleeved shirt, a hand axe in a holster hanging down one leg. If he was pissed at having been taken away from his real work to answer the same questions again, he didn't show it.

"So what have we got?"

Rick waved toward the cliff edge.

"Waiting for final permission before we start. I'm supposed to answer any questions you have about whether the agreed distance to this cliff is enough to cover safety requirements."

That surprised Laura. From her careful reading of state logging regulations, she knew it would take more than the opinion of a logging foreman to verify what Rick was talking about.

"Haven't a soil scientist and a geologist already given their opinions?"

"No. They'll be out soon. I've worked with the state geologist before, and he wanted me to take an informal look and tell him how likely it was that he'd have to make a tough call. Then he'll know how much time he needs to spend here. Seems they've got several projects in the works and they're stretched thin…"

He reflected a moment.

"… I don't think it's a tough call."

She relaxed a bit. Looking over the shoulder of an informal assessment was a lot more within her level of competence than participating in a decision that would become very public.

They both knew the larger issue they'd just skirted. Four years after the disaster at Gideon, it was still a touchstone issue and the media had thick files on what happened there.

49

Gideon, an old self-sufficient settlement, had seen an influx of new residents as Seattle's high tech development began to have secondary effects on housing prices. First Microsoft, then others, turned from small operations into juggernauts dominating the east side of Lake Washington. Seattle and Bellevue got most of the big surge. Later, communities farther out, like Gideon, felt the backwash of urban change.

People who couldn't afford Seattle and Bellevue, then Everett and Bellingham, went farther away to settle. Developers built houses the buyers could afford, which meant construction with less substantial materials to go along with cheaper prices.

The backers of the Isadka Valley project—30 miles southeast of Gideon—were well aware of public opinion. They'd taken every required step, and even a few that weren't strictly required, to demonstrate that they had complied with all legal and environmental provisions. Exercising such caution, they'd already lost several months in their projected schedule and now wanted to move ahead without delay.

Rick glanced back over his shoulder at the precipice both of them knew they were talking about. Laura could hear the rushing water in the river below. They were on a tributary of the Skagit River, which started in Canada then flowed south into Washington, where it turned west and exited into Puget Sound.

Rick turned his gaze back to her and made a waving motion. She saw the impatience in it.

"I'm a forester foreman, that's all. It's not for me to say which requirements are needed or not. I just want to get this puppy moving."

"I'm with you on that. But besides the scientific okay, people are still wondering about ownership. You know, because of Gideon."

Rick frowned and looked away. She was not surprised. No one wanted to open that can of worms. However, there was no way to move the puppy without examining the worms. She almost laughed at the mixed image, but her levity came and went in an instant. The ownership issue was neither a metaphor nor a joke.

While reading all she could about the Gideon slide, a minor story had caught her attention. There was some evidence, or a rumor

50

that one reporter thought worth tracking down, that ownership of the Gideon site was not clear. Officially, the site above the slide area consisted of a number of separate parcels, all under twenty acres each. The article hinted that perhaps a single business interest controlled all those sites.

If the disaster there could be explained as only an act of God, some leniency in the regulations made sense for small parcels and the tribes. But if a single interest was hiding behind those separate parcels, no politician would back anything but strict, unvarying oversight of all new logging sites.

Rick seemed to read her mind.

"This project's clean. The land used to be owned by a large forestry company. It was bought by some financial outfit in New York and now belongs to the University of Washington. The University reviews proposals from investors, the two parties sign a contract, and then it's the investors who have to get all the permits. They've done that. Everything is one contiguous tract, except this part right here where we are, and one other small section on the upper side of the tract. Both of those include independently-owned parcels."

"You know it's the independently owned parcels people will be looking at."

There it was, out in the open. Rick stared at her with undisguised unease, then pulled back.

"Okay. That's all from me."

"You know more?"

"If I do, I'm staying out of it."

"C'mon, Rick. Whatever you know, it's going to come out. Tell me now and I can report to people who can check. You said you want a decision. If what they find is okay, the project'll go forward quicker. We're talking your job here. You should want to help clear the air."

She heard herself and flinched at the tone of her voice. Something was bothering this guy, but all she could think of was the goal and the most direct way to achieve it. She should have stayed calmer, listened more.

"Yeah, I got a job, and I also got a family. They come first."

She tried to sound concerned.

"You're saying you're scared for your family?"

"Didn't say that."

"Not what you said, but how you said it."

She'd let sharpness creep back despite her resolve. She waited.

After a moment, he wavered.

"Curt Longcart."

"Curt Longcart? The car dealer in Shoreline, the guy with those irritating commercials? Is there another one?"

"No. Same guy."

"What's he got to do with this project?"

"That's it. There's got to be a record somewhere. You go find it. People ask me, I never even knew Longcart was involved."

He waved generally at the trees around them.

"Besides, another guy's coming to ask me the same questions. Why don't you state guys get together and do everything at once instead of wasting my time over and over?"

The friendliness was gone, and so was Rick. He turned and strode back into the woods.

❋ ❋ ❋

After Rick walked away, Laura stood still, looking down at the rushing river below and the forest on the other bank. What had her talk with Rick produced? Nothing, really, but a name and an impression that there was important information still to be found. And she wasn't even the person to go forward with it. All she could do was report the conversation and let others figure out what a car salesman had to do with it all.

She took her time walking back to her car, gradually shedding the weight of her thoughts. It didn't take long for her to lengthen her stride. The scent of the forest seeped in, and she dropped into the familiar rhythm of exercise.

Her mind was nearly blank when she registered the shape of her car and then a person standing next to it.

A natural impulse to flee was her first reaction. But where could she go except back into the forest? This guy was both big and, from the looks of him, in good shape. No one to turn your back on. She kept on walking toward her car as if he wasn't there. He stepped away and spoke.

"Hi. I'm Gary Seasons and I work for OPUS, One Puget Sound, the governor's new…"

"I know what OPUS is."

Her interjection sounded challenging. Not what she intended.

"Good. I heard some of what you and Rick Groff were talking about."

She flared.

"You listened in?"

"Just enough to get the drift and realize that we're both here for the same reason. Once I knew that, I stopped listening and came here to wait for you to finish."

Laura calmed down. His face and name tugged at her memory.

"You're the football player."

"I was, now I'm with OPUS."

His past didn't mean that much to her. She was no football fan, but she knew that football players were the most financially well-supported and coddled athletes at the U. Was this guy another one of those? She hesitated, and he must have noticed.

"Does my past life as a jock present a problem for you?"

"No. I competed, too. Crew."

He paused and thought.

"I used to watch regattas. You're Laura Dickens. The four seat in the number one boat?"

"That's me."

He smiled.

She rolled her eyes.

"Okay, I hope we got that over with."

He smiled again and gave a casual shrug.

"Let's see if we're on the same page about this place. The question is whether the state will issue a logging permit. A couple of environmental evaluations are missing, but from what I hear, those are going to come in favorable. That leaves the issue of approval for several small parcels in the mix. You know, the Gideon situation."

She recognized what was going on. As former jocks, they both had to fight the perception that they were less prepared than "serious" analysts. She had already decided he wasn't dumb, and both of them were after the same information. The essential thing was to get on with the job. She relaxed and added an encouraging smile.

"That's how it seems to me, too."

"Okay. I came here to talk to Rick, but you got to him first. You willing to tell me what he told you?"

Bureaucracies, Laura was learning, were very conscious of boundaries. As a newcomer, it might be best to be careful. She did a quick calculation. Sharing information at this level should be okay.

"I think Rick wants this project to move ahead. But he seemed a little nervous about the ownership matter."

"Did he say why?"

"Not exactly."

"Meaning..."

"He mentioned a man who might have some connection to the project. Or some connection to what made him nervous. Curt Long-cart, the used-car guy. Don't know why that would be important."

Laura could see that Gary was startled, maybe even shaken.

"You know him?"

"Too well."

"Can you give me something to pass on up the line?"

Gary crossed his arms and looked deeper into the forest. Eventually he nodded.

"Let's find a place where we can talk. There's no short answer."

❋ ❋ ❋

Gary signaled, watched Laura put on her blinker behind him, and pulled into a turnoff. He didn't want to take any chance of being recognized in a coffee shop.

A bench faced a low wall, beyond which you could look out over undisturbed forests toward the south as far as you could see. "Undisturbed" meant you still couldn't detect signs of the clear-cut logging that had chopped holes in the original wild green carpet. It also meant ignoring the far corner of the view where urban sprawl began—a sprawl that extended, pretty much unbroken, from there all the way south to Olympia. He'd enjoy as much solace and sense of place as he could, and ignore what he had to edit out.

He walked to the bench and Laura joined him. He looked her over, hoping the survey wasn't too obvious. He guessed her to be around five-ten, with the broad shoulders and solid frame you'd expect on a rower: She was dressed in logger's boots, jeans, and a zip-up jacket with a State of Washington logo below her left shoulder. Her short-cut light brown hair moved with the breeze.

Though he'd stood near her a few minutes ago, he couldn't remember her eye color. That wasn't the kind of thing that registered with him. But he had noted the impression she gave off, of someone who focused seriously on the tasks in front of her.

They sat on the bench, each of them closer to an end than to the middle. Traffic on the highway was widely spaced but steady. He took one more look at the view and adjusted his position with one arm across the back rest, half turning so he could look at her. She was already looking at him, waiting for him to begin.

"Curt Longcart."

She nodded.

"Okay. So he's known for Longcart Motors in Lynnwood. His dad actually started the business, but Curt made it more than just a stop on Route 99. Later, he took the business statewide, then even into Idaho."

She gave him a speed-up sign.

"That's important, because Curt likes to pretend he's a folksy small-time used car dealer. You probably know the ads—that dumb trio, the Triplets on late-night TV. But he's involved in much more than cars, and he's no yokel."

"Go on."

"Behind the public image, Curt's a small conglomerate. He speculates, in real estate mostly, and also in timber."

"He's done all that with profits from car sales?"

"Good question, and the answer could affect both of our investigations. At the beginning it was car money. Curt did okay, but not all that well. Real estate is always a crap shoot. As a solo investor, he made some mistakes. Around 2004, he started working with partners. Some of his connections were with the tribes."

"I'll make a guess. Because he's part Indian."

"You must watch his commercials."

"Not that much, but it's obvious what he wants you to see."

"Right. It may be that he actually has Indian blood. Hard to tell. I've been around him a lot, and he's never offered any details on his heritage. One thing is true: He tried to get the area around his original location designated as a reservation."

"I didn't know that. Let me guess. Because tribal land is exempt from some federal control. Good for a tax break and profits."

"Right. The issue is technically still pending, but I doubt it's going anywhere. Others have tried the same thing, and the larger tribes oppose any expansion of tribal areas unless it's theirs. Regardless, Curt increased his involvement with the tribes, particularly in timber leases."

"Now we're getting to it. Go on."

He paused to figure how to present the next part.

"Look. From here on I'm close to hearsay, with not a lot to back it up other than innuendo and guesses. Curt likes to play the fool so a buyer'll think there's no problem getting a sweet deal from ol' Curt. But he's a lot smarter than that."

She frowned and her voice got sharper.

"I understand, but if that's all you've got—innuendo and guesses—then I don't think there's much value in continuing."

"No, there's more. I didn't want to over-promise. What I have's not provable."

Laura's shoulders dropped. She took a long breath, and let it out almost like a sigh.

"Okay, what is it?"

"When I was at the U, my main focus was football. I stayed with studies enough to complete three and a half years toward a degree so I could finish it later—which I did."

A note of pride crept in. When she didn't react, he went on.

"It was like I had a third job, too. Curt wanted my notoriety, and he was constantly after me to come to his dealership. I didn't have the time, and I ducked his requests a lot. But sometimes I couldn't."

"Couldn't? How did he make you come?"

He rearranged his position and shook his head.

"No details, okay, but he'd helped me during high school in a way that was potentially, let's say, embarrassing."

He hurried on, fencing out any more questions on that topic.

"Anyway, when I was there Curt would trot me out at events. He'd tell everyone he'd given me a job because, as he said over and over, 'I'm not just interested in cars. I do my best to see that people get a good deal in life.' Humble bullshit is one of good ol' Curt's prime acts."

She grimaced. He'd wandered from the subject.

"How does this relate to that parcel we just left?"

"I was getting there. So one of my private visits with him during college was after a kegger put on by a UDub booster club. Curt had had a few. He hunched in like we might be overheard, even though the room was emptying out. His eyes were glazed, but mostly he was excited. He told me about a meeting he had the day before."

Gary cleared his voice, looked carefully at Laura, and tried for a firm lock on her eyes.

"Before I say more, tell me again what you'll do with it."

"Depends on what you say. And how much I can attribute to you."

"Right. Can we agree on no attribution at all unless I tell you it's okay?"

"If you tell me someone was murdered, I couldn't do that."

He allowed a small laugh.

"No murder. But there might be enough for you and others in your office to follow up. Curt told me that he was making an investment in timber that would have a huge payoff. Said that his 'secret sauce'—he talks that way—would 'make the deal real tasty.' I took that to mean he

57

was fixing the deal in some way. I'd seen him do that many times, like it was second nature."

"Is that it?"

He couldn't miss the disappointment.

"The deal was for the Gideon parcel."

Her eyes shot open.

"What? I read most of the records about it. I never saw Longcart's name anywhere."

"Doesn't surprise me. In fact, it's what I would have expected. Curt likes deals where he is a silent partner. Maybe 'hidden' is a better word."

"Do you have proof?"

"Like I said, me personally, no. There's an old rumor that proof might exist: a recording of a conversation where someone said things that were never supposed to be public. The rumor popped up immediately after the big slide. Then it disappeared. That's why I was surprised when I heard it again about two weeks ago."

"That's interesting. But, as you said, no more than rumor, for now. What made you want to tell me?"

There was a hint of an accusation there. He tried to stay even and reasonable.

"I don't think it would do any good for me to press Curt. With me, his first move would be to ramp up his threat to punish me for our arrangement ten years ago. I was thinking that if someone in your office investigated, maybe confronted him about the rumor, he'd overreact. Maybe make a mistake that could help us figure out what's going on."

She kept silent, waiting. When he didn't say anything more, she nodded without looking at him.

"Okay, Gary. Thanks for the heads-up. Like you say, that's not much to go on. But if I think of something, I'll let you know."

He had a quick idea.

"May make sense for us to keep in touch on others things, too. We're both working on Isadka Valley. We'll save a lot of hassle if we can avoid duplication."

She smiled that she understood. He watched her leave. Her straight back gave no indication whether she picked up that "staying in touch" could mean more than just avoiding duplicated work.

He remained where he was, facing the southern view. Laura's car started, and he listened to the engine sound fade. He did okay with male athletes, coaches, and bosses. Dealing with just about everyone else was a mystery.

❄ ❄ ❄

Grant Tomson laced up his boots, added a vest to the protection of a heavy wool shirt, and stepped out into a late afternoon merging with dusk. Dark green firs looked black against a background of light drizzle and drifting mist. Low-lying bushes were like bundles of bristles, bare of leaves. He'd been to this place several times over the last ten years, and this was the first time he'd seen the cabin's roof without some snow on it in early November.

The familiar scene felt alien without its white blanket. As he walked briskly along a damp trail, sentinel Doug firs crowded him on both sides, and, as usual, he compared wherever he was to his varied commercial enterprises. They, too, were being crowded, not by stationary objects like trees, but by shifting human behavior.

God how he resented that. He knew what he wanted, what he needed to do. Most of what he did with his life was no one else's business. He didn't mind competitors. They got his juices flowing. But bureaucrats, regulators, lawyers, the media. Drown all of them, and the world would be a better place. His world, for sure. What right did anyone have to mess with his family's affairs up at the lake? Or to second guess an investment that would drive the local economy forward? What happened between him and his brother was family business, no one else's.

It didn't help that over the last couple of weeks he'd noticed an uptick in the number of times his name was being searched for on the net. What did that mean? What if someone had the tape, and unseen forces were moving against him?

There was no evidence that that tape had passed beyond the Flanerty girl. But she might have decided to use it against him. Never mind that it was unlikely she knew that he was involved. Other people listening to the tape would figure that out

The Isadka project was moving at a glacial pace and his isolation was in the middle of the glacier. That's the way he felt, cooped up inside the cabin. That feeling usually left him during his walks, but today it hadn't. If anything it had grown stronger.

He had to do something to combat the inertia. Whatever the outcome, he'd feel better doing something. Without thinking further think he reversed his path and was soon back at the cabin.

As he was unlocking the door, he heard his cell phone pinging. At least his phone connection hadn't deserted him.

He punched on and recognized the voice.

"We've found her."

NOVEMBER 8

Key was back from work at the bar. She didn't need to look at her watch to know it was after 1:00 a.m. Her big table was its usual mess. One item caught her attention. She lifted the pad on which Crash had written his email address and cell number, and stared at it just long enough to realize all that it meant. Immediately she dropped it, as if it had seared her skin.

The place was hers again—only it wasn't. A sense of Crash having been here hung in the air like an alien presence.

A fucked-up life was all she'd known until Walt took her in. Then she'd had a peek at a new way of living, safe and predictable. They were only glimpses, though—like tasting food you liked, only to discover that a glass pane stood between you and getting more. In stray moments she'd begun to hope that the pane would eventually shatter. She'd even started to trust that it would, and let down her guard. Big mistake. Suspicion and vigilance were the only permanent answers.

She hadn't seen or heard anything of the mysterious motorcycle, but one thing was clear: If Crash had found her, so could others. Walt's idea of having her stay here had been crazy from the start. Now it had become dangerous.

She assessed the items on the table. She'd keep the iPad and the phone. She'd transfer all of her files onto one hard drive and destroy the rest. Some of the binders on the shelf would have to be burned. Everything else, she'd leave where it was. Once started, she could be gone in a few hours. She wouldn't tell Walt's lawyer. Sorting it all out would be his concern.

That left one important item, the cause of it all: her dad's tape. It shouldn't stay here in the house. Walt had asked if she'd checked on it, and she'd been truthful in saying she hadn't. Before anything else, she ought to make sure it was still safe.

Two years ago, she'd finally told Walt about the tape. He'd been the one who suggested making two more versions and hiding all of them. One would be the real item. The two copies would begin just like the real one—her father's voice interspersed with short responses from the man he was talking to—but would stop after four minutes of minor conversation before the important part started.

Key thought then, and still did, that the copies were an unnecessary gimmick. But Walt read a lot of mysteries and was enjoying himself, so she played along. Walt chose the places to hide the copies. Only Key knew where she hid the real tape.

To reassure herself, she decided to check on them. Walt had been right to be careful, but she'd seen no signs of intruders for days now. That ought to make a quick inspection safe enough.

She climbed to the master bedroom on the second floor. The bed was neatly made, covered with a hand-stitched quilt that had some kind of family history. Walt had occupied that room until he got too ill to climb the stairs. Nobody had disturbed it since then. That included a worn Turkish carpet, beneath which was a loose floorboard that could be easily removed. In the space below it, a searcher would find one of the incomplete tapes. Walt suggested making one of the versions easy to find so searchers would not for further. But there were others.

She entered the room's walk-in closet, pulled a hanging light cord, and looked up at the ceiling. Another shorter cord was attached to a square wood panel covering an attic access. She had to get a straight-back chair to reach that cord and pull it. A panel hinged downward, revealing a folded ladder. She lowered herself off the chair and shoved it away to make room for the now extended ladder.

At the top of the ladder, she reached into her pocket for a small flashlight and moved the beam around. The attic was sparsely filled with bric-a-brac, suitcases, a steamer trunk, and scattered cardboard boxes. Most of them belonged to Walt. Others she'd filled with junk items that she found in the trash at the AlkiSteel mill. In one of them, she'd hidden the second decoy tape. It was unwrapped and looked pretty much like the junk around it. She had to rummage in the junk before she found it was still there.

Then she retrieved a short stepladder from behind the steamer trunk. Her flashlight beam found exposed roof supports connected horizontally by 2x6 stringers. She counted from one end and placed the ladder under one of the stringers. Climbing up, she felt around the metal flanges that connected the stringer to a vertical support. Her fingers found what she was searching for: the original tape, snugly wrapped in duct tape, glued to a gray metal flange. From below it was invisible.

She replaced the ladder and retraced her path to the bedroom below, checking to make sure there were no signs that she had recently been there.

Back in her basement, she reviewed her decision to leave. Still a good idea, but maybe not right now. There was no imminent danger that she could tell, and just knowing that the tape was safe took some pressure off. She'd give herself a couple of days to sift through her belongings and files. Then she'd be gone.

Only one thing made her uncomfortable: She had to tell Walt. He'd done a lot for her, and she owed him that much. She'd pay him another visit and tell him she'd gotten a job in another city. He could figure out a different way to dispose of his house and other assets.

She'd be doing what she wanted. She'd travel lighter, get rid of more stuff. She could keep up with her blogging, or change it, or ditch it completely. None of that really mattered.

She had no worries about Crash or his feelings. But she didn't want him checking up on her. And he would, if she didn't move fast enough.

Settled, then. Now she really did feel better.

The clock read 4 am. Time to sleep.

❄ ❄ ❄

After a few hours that felt like restless minutes, Crash couldn't locate sleep again. The same thing had happened last night and the night before. Seeing Key again merged with memories of his time back at the UDub boarding house.

There he'd slept less than his other housemates, and was usually the last one to bed. But on some nights, as the house quieted, he'd sense that someone else was also awake. That would be Key. She'd stay in her room until the noises stopped. Then she'd go down to the living room or the kitchen and sit there absorbed with her computer. If he walked in on her, she wouldn't acknowledge him.

But he couldn't help it. He liked watching her, this small, enclosed creature, much prettier than the long bangs over her eyes and the formless clothes she wore allowed others to see. Even after she'd disappeared, he still felt drawn to her.

In the intervening years, images of her had returned at odd moments. Less frequently as time went on, but still there. Finding her again started up old feelings, but he had no idea what they meant or where they would lead. That didn't bother him; he started almost everything with incomplete information and an unknown destination. He began to doze.

Suddenly his cell phone yanked him back to consciousness. He fumbled for it, punched on, and heard words so garbled that he figured it was a wrong number or that the speaker was high on something. He almost hung up, then realized it was Key.

"Key. I hear you, but I can't understand you. Slow down and speak up."

He had to repeat the same words, raising his voice, before something intelligible broke through her crazed whisper.

"Someone...in house. Maybe more than one."

"Where are you? Are you safe?"

"Basement...hiding."

"Where are they?"

"Upstairs...oh no."

Crash heard a door burst open, and the phone went dead.

Still in the T-shirt and sweatpants he slept in, Crash ran to his car. He raced down I-5 and across the West Seattle Bridge in less than fifteen minutes.

At the end of the bridge he turned two corners before speeding through the mill's parking area and onto the gravel driveway toward Key's house. In front of the shed-like garage, he slid to a halt and left the car where it was. Grabbing a flashlight from the glove compartment, he ran toward the house as dawn began to creep up over its steep roof. The upper stories were lit and the front door was wide open.

His heart sunk. Key would never leave the door open. Moving quickly but carefully, he cracked open the door to the basement and listened. Nothing. He opened it all the way and stepped through. Still nothing. So he closed the door behind him and took the steps down two at a time.

In the glare of overhead lights, Crash walked around the space, taking in the work and kitchen areas. Drawers had been emptied and binders knocked off the shelves. Through the open door to the bedroom he saw a double bed with clothes strewn around it. On his knees, he checked under the bed. Nothing.

He returned to the main room.

"Key, it's me, Crash. Are you here?"

At first he heard nothing. Then there was a noise, almost like a whimper. He couldn't place its location.

"If that's you, Key, tell me where you are."

Then he heard a voice but couldn't make out the words. It was coming from the corner with the hot water tank. He moved closer.

"...other...people...here. Are we... alone?"

He kept his voice low to match hers.

"I don't think there's anyone else here. No car but mine. The front door was open, but I didn't see or hear anyone. If you want, I'll go check."

"No. Stay!"

The voice came from behind the water heater. There was just enough space on either side of it for a very small person to squeeze behind and hide.

"Okay. But we're trapped down here. Even if someone's upstairs we'd have a better chance trying to get away now."

There was a long pause.

"I thought I heard them leave after I called you."

"Them? More than one?"

"I heard voices talking."

"Wait."

As quietly as possible, he climbed the basement stairs and listened at the closed door. He waited a good two minutes before easing the door open, listening again, and then coming back down.

"No voices, and I didn't hear anything else."

"Maybe they found it and left."

67

Then he saw her, flattened against the wall and edging out from behind the big tank. Her hair was full of dust, and he could see spider webs on the shoulders and arms of her dark pullover.

Once out from behind the tank, Key froze. Crash saw terror on her face.

"You want me to check the rest of the house?"

She nodded, and as he moved, she followed. Halfway up the basement stairs, she stopped. Crash threw caution to the winds and rushed through a surface check of the two floors above.

He found no one, amid unmistakable evidence that intruders had been there. Every drawer had been pulled out and dumped. The mattress in the master bedroom was on the floor, covered with clothes from the closet. One of its sides was slit open. The rug had been pulled back, revealing an out-of-place board and an empty space below it. In the closet, he saw a pull-down ladder extending into the attic. He climbed up, scanned the attic space, and climbed back down.

Then he rushed back to Key.

She stood by the kitchen sink, splashing water on her face over and over. The movement was so repetitive that she looked like a large wind-up toy. Finally, she stopped and dried off with a dish towel. When she glanced at him she looked paler than usual, and her hands trembled. She stood, swaying slightly, then let out a long breath and slumped into one of the chairs by the kitchen table. He sat in one of the others and waited. When he thought she might be able to focus, he spoke.

"They could be just thieves. There've been a lot of break-ins on Delridge and some in West Seattle."

She shook her head.

"They were looking for the tape. They wanted proof."

"Proof of what?"

"My dad was a logging foreman. He found out about a scam management was working, and he taped a conversation, I guess for protection later if he needed it."

She was in a kind of trance. He waited for more. When she was ready, she went on.

"He never told me that he was protecting himself with the tape. I just guessed that. He gave it to me one day, said to guard it and never tell anyone I had it. A month ago my uncle called to tell me my dad was killed in an accident. At least, it seemed like an accident. I don't believe it was."

"Maybe we should listen to that tape."

She shook her head.

"Gimme a moment."

She turned away and Crash sat back to wait when her phone started buzzing. She let four repetitions pass before she punched on, walking toward a corner.

A few moments later he heard "I'll come." She turned toward him and sagged. Her face couldn't hide shock and sorrow.

It took her a while to produce words.

"That was the nursing home. Walt fell out of his bed. They've taken him to the hospital. He's losing it."

❋ ❋ ❋

Crash tried once more to draw Key into conversation, but a hospital waiting room didn't encourage talk. Most people were either leafing through magazines or staring into space. Finally, a couple occupying a couch in an alcove left, and he moved quickly to gain a little privacy. Key hesitated, then followed.

Crash lifted a knee and pivoted to face her.

"You've done all you can. Want to tell me more about Walter?"

"I already told you. He took me in. Let me stay in his place."

He thought she would remain silent, but she went on in an introspective voice that sounded almost alien, coming from her.

"There are two Walters. Only a few people know that. One's the successful business guy. He gave people around him a lot of freedom. He gave second chances if they made mistakes, but he'd fire them if they tried to take advantage of him. Some people in the company were known as 'Walter's guys.' They'd do anything for him. That's why I could stay in the house after he went to the nursing home. They

69

kept the electricity and water flowing, kept the car serviced. That kinda shit."

"And the other Walter?"

"Privately, he was real radical. So was his wife, before she died. They did things secretly. Walter once told me the way to live was to do what you're good at, get paid for doing it, and then use your money to do real good. He knew he was good at business, though he didn't much like his job. He got satisfaction by giving money to causes, gay rights, political candidates, private social service groups. That kinda thing."

"You were interested in those causes?"

"Yeah, enough I guess, along with other things where we saw eye to eye. We found out about that gradually. After the first night he took me in, he began quizzing me. It was a conversation that repeated over several weeks. That was real new for me. I wasn't, you know, too communicative."

Key glanced his way with the closest thing to a smile he'd seen for a while. He gave her a big encouraging one in return. She sank into thought, though her expression lightened a little. He prodded.

"So you were one of his projects?"

A tiny smile again.

"Yeah, I guess you could say so. But he never made me feel that way. After a while I felt more like a partner than a project. There were times I looked for proof he might be trying to take charge of me, you know. But I never found any."

They might have gone on longer, but a doctor arrived wearing a professional, solicitous expression. He delivered words he'd obviously used before.

"We did our best, but I'm sorry to say that Mr. Vickers did not make it. His condition was too weak to fight off the effects of the head trauma. He passed without regaining consciousness."

He finished with a stock condolence and left.

Crash concentrated on Key, ready to help her. But she showed the hard face of someone who willed all emotion away. She didn't even look at him when she spoke.

"Gotta move. Things to do."

70

She stood up and walked quickly away.

He caught up with her in the parking garage. Dawn was breaking. Through openings on the Sound side of the structure he could see sunshine just touching the tops of the Olympics. Key looked around, temporarily bewildered.

"Forgot where I left my car."

"That's because we came in mine."

"Oh yeah."

She might just blow him off, but he had to try.

"C'mon, I'll take you."

She glared, suspicion unmistakable on her face. Then her focus moved toward the Olympics, and she nicked a nod.

"Just home, then you leave."

He said nothing.

❈ ❈ ❈

Again in the big house by the mill—hers now if she wanted it—Key reassessed everything.

While Crash was driving, she'd checked voice messages. There was only one, from a nurse at Alki View, Walt's retirement home.

"I didn't want to intrude on your grief. But…something happened in the hours before your friend took a turn for the worse last night. I was at my station and heard a strange sound. When I checked around and found your friend on the floor, I got an aide to help me get him up on the bed and called a doctor…"

Key heard a breath intake, then the nurse went on.

"I looked around and found a ground floor window open near the kitchen. It shouldn't have been open, and it wasn't when my shift started. I went right to the night manager, but she didn't want me to tell anyone else what I found. See, she didn't want to have to report to the county. That meant more work for her. I don't know what you want to do about it, but I thought you ought to know."

Too late, she realized that the speaker was on. With the silence in the car, Key knew Crash had been able to hear the nurse too. He looked at her, alarmed, the second she hung up.

She shivered. The warning was unmistakable. If Walt had been in danger, she, Key, might be too. People could be out there watching the house right now.

Once they arrived, Crash took charge. Before she quite realized what was happening, he'd packed her clothes and toiletries. Now a bulging knapsack stood there beside him.

She hadn't been herself, what with Walter's death, and she had clearly lost her vigilance. When she finally realized what Crash had done, she snapped at him.

"That's it. You leave! I don't need your help."

He's like a leech, she thought. There he was, standing by the door, arms crossed. Confident. That's what got her the most. She put on her most dangerous expression.

Crash spoke but didn't move.

"I have no intention of leaving you alone right now. Especially after the nurse's call. I'm sticking with you until you're safe. So better get used to it."

Where did that come from? His goofy smile was gone. He had assumed his familiar forward-leaning hunch, but now his legs were planted. She revised her previous opinion: This wasn't the same push-over she'd known.

"No way."

"Look at your choices. You have to get out of here, and arguing with me is wasting time."

Key had to admit she couldn't physically get around him. He wasn't big, but all of a sudden he projected a strength that surprised her, and he was right—they were wasting time. She tried to think of another way around. Nothing good occurred. So she fell back to a familiar threat.

"You're going to pay for this later."

Those words sounded feeble, even to her.

Crash said nothing. He waited while she grabbed her iPad and hard drives and tossed them in a backpack. That was all she needed—except for one more thing.

"I've gotta get something from upstairs."

She ran up to the master bedroom. In the attic, it took very little time to climb up and break the glued bond between that small wrapped package and the rafter.

Crash hadn't moved from his station by the front door. She could tell he hadn't missed a thing.

As they exited the house, Key took note of the broken lock on the front door and reminded herself to call Walt's lawyer when she could. She was also conscious of the tape in her backpack. She could almost feel the heat, like a hot brick she didn't want to touch, much less carry around. She decided to take a chance.

"Wait here."

Crash was stuffing bags into the car. When she spoke, he took a step in her direction.

"No! I said wait."

She entered the garage, rushed through and exited from a small door at the rear. Dense growth abutted a wall that separated the company property from the houses beyond. Walt had built a lean-to against the rear side of the garage for a huge old tractor that had once belonged to his folks. It was by now a piece of junk. Its tall rubber tires had been flat for years.

The tractor's motor was behind hinged lift-up panels. She dropped her knapsack, pulled out the small wrapped tape and lifted one of the panels. By feel, she found a horizontal flange under the engine that would do. She worked quickly and in less than a minute trotted back to the car. Without a word, both climbed in.

Crash drove above the speed limit, and she didn't interrupt to ask where they were going.

His route took them south into Burien, where the side streets had little traffic. He alternately slowed and sped up, his eyes frequently on the rearview mirror. Once he spoke briefly.

"So far, no one's following."

For the next forty minutes he made sure. Where 148th met State 509, he turned north, exited at his next opportunity, made a small loop on side streets, and returned to State 503, this time taking the exit toward SeaTac Airport. He passed the airport and continued east until the road joined I-405 north.

With frequent lane shifts, they wove through the heavy traffic around Bellevue. Several miles later he went south at the junction with I-5 until he reached 50th Street. They'd gone more than 40 miles, Key realized, making a circle around the Seattle metro area.

Driving south through Wallingford, with the ship canal getting closer, Crash took a sharp right into the yard of a building that advertised construction materials. Once parked, he shut off the car and smiled.

"Finally here. C'mon, I'll show you what that means."

❋ ❋ ❋

Crash knew his place would be a real comedown from the size and convenience of the big house where Key had been living. He hastily explained the situation. The owner was waiting for the housing market to pick up so he could build more apartments. In the interim, a friend of Crash's ran a concrete, slate, and sidewalk business out of an old warehouse on the property. Piles of slate and pavers were stacked in the open, and thieves had discovered them. So it was win-win to let Crash live for free in a small outbuilding, in return for checking on the stacked materials a couple of times during the night.

The outbuilding had electricity and a closet-like toilet and sink. The rest of its space was cut in two by a temporary plywood divider. The larger part contained a hotplate, a table, and a second-hand lounger. A queen-size mattress was on the floor in the smaller area. The knee-length raincoat that, except during the warmest summer months, was his year-round outer garment hung from a nail on one wall. Both rooms had oil space heaters. He used a shower in the main warehouse, and had a key for an outside door. This arrangement had panned out just fine for the last seven months.

"Okay, here's the deal."

Key listened stonily, arms crossed, not moving away from the door to the outside.

74

"You can have the mattress in the small room. I'll sleep on the lounger. I'll pound in a couple of nails so you can hang up things. We eat here at this little table. You get the straight chair, and I'll sit on the edge of the lounger. Kinda cramped, but we'll get by. I'll come up with something better in a few days."

He wondered when she would make a move, say something, anything. Finally she did, dropping her knapsack and sitting in the chair. She looked around, not hiding her disgust.

"Who would ever choose to live in this hole?'

"I know it's not for everyone. Suits me, though."

"Why?"

That was an accusation, not a question. But at least she was talking, not getting set to run away.

"I saw what it means to want to have it all. It's a trip with a destination you never reach. I decided to try for a lot of small destinations, and simple ways to reach them. 'Simple' basically means no baggage."

"Jeez, profound. But bullshit is still bullshit. How do you get the money? Or are you one of those who doesn't have to work? If you are, you could live better than this."

"No family wealth. I'm on my own. I do have jobs, one as a night watchman here, and I clean up at a glass art studio."

"Glass studio?"

"Yeah, it's not far from here. I'll show you later."

"Do I have to put on my leash?"

He let that one pass.

"You must be hungry. There's a Pizza & More a couple of blocks away."

"I'm good."

He stayed between her and the door. No use in making a move now. She went into the tiny bathroom, then into the space beyond the partition.

NOVEMBER 9

Key wasn't sure how long she slept. Daylight ringed the shade over a window. When she rose she ached all over.

All she remembered from before was looking at the mattress and thinking how it had looked like a welcome mat. Then, that she'd dropped her backpack and lay down, intending to wait Crash out.

When she opened the door to the larger room, Crash was standing near the door. Only the bagels and coffee on the table told her that he had moved from that position sometime since she last saw him.

They ate in silence until Crash spoke.

"You want to talk about your blogging?"

That surprised her. Key was wary.

"Why?"

"It interests me, that's all. Get to know me a little better and you'll see that's what drives me—chasing what's interesting. I gave up the straight and narrow so I could do that."

She made a small snort.

"Get to know you better? Never happen. I've got interests, too, and you're not one of them."

"Like posting at mittandhiss?"

She jumped up, an arm extended and pointing.

"You hacked me. You and the others. That's it. Don't try to stop me."

She raised her backpack. He stepped forward and grabbed the other shoulder strap.

"Take it easy. You're safe. Please. You'd be in more danger out on the streets."

She pulled harder but he held tight.

"You're mad? Yeah, I found your blog, okay? But I didn't hack you or anything. That first time in your basement, I saw a printed doc with 'mittandhiss' on it. I just searched for it and found the blog. That's all."

"You followed me home that night, and then you spied on me online. That's messed up."

He sighed.

"A little, yeah, I guess. I didn't mean to freak you out. I'm sorry. I was just really curious, you know? I keep up with the tech world, too. So, what should I call you? Yavay or Shluss?"

That got her. With one arm, she grabbed her knapsack again. The other hand slapped him hard. He kept his head as far away as he could as he held down her arms. He was a lot stronger than he looked.

"You need to hear the rest."

"Let go of me! Now! I'm leaving."

He loosened his grip, but not enough for her to squirm away.

"Hear me out, Key."

Maybe it was the urgent tone in his voice, or just exhaustion and fear combining to weaken her. She stopped struggling.

He let go a bit more.

"I know you'd rather not be here, but this is as safe a place as you're going to find. I want to show you what's important. Once I've done that, if you still want to leave, I won't stand in your way. I promise. Deal?"

She was shaking with anger. He was so damned insistent. Why did he care so much? She didn't want to be here, but where else did she have to go? And part of her wanted to know what he knew.

She managed a nod.

But there was something else: To her surprise, she felt a prick of curiosity.

❈ ❈ ❈

Crash looked up from his computer to find Key focused on the screen as he typed.

"How do you do that?"

She took a step toward him, close enough that he could have counted the colorful beads on the bracelet she always wore. Interest had erased her habitual scowl.

"Do what?"

"Move so fast. It's like you're changing to another screen before you read what's on the first one."

"Habit. Just do it, I guess."

"Well, what are you looking at, and how did a slacker like you get so good with computers?"

He swiveled to face her.

"Okay, second question first. That's the easy one. My parents are scientists, a doctor and an engineer. They sent me to a lot of special courses and camps, mostly for computers. I was a computer science major at MIT for two years, then UDub for one before I dropped out. I went to MIT because it was what my parents wanted. By the end of my sophomore year I was burnt out and tried UDub."

She sat and he waved around the tiny space where they sat.

"After that I followed other interests."

He went back to the screen, and she stayed quiet. It didn't take long for him to have something to show her.

"Here you are, Klooch."

She leaned in, then reared back. She was looking at a post she'd written about ten days earlier, under the alias Klooch.

"Shit. How'd you do that? I never let people know who I am."

"You don't hide as well as you think."

Now Key was insulted.

"What's that supposed to mean?"

"Nothing personal. I'm just trying to help. Look: If I found you, so can someone else. You can't stay anonymous."

"Okay. But what's the big deal? I'm only blogging, like a hobby, you know."

He decided to give her all of it. There would be a price to pay, but protecting her was worth it.

"I think we both know it's more than just a hobby. You're not just some random blogger. There's passion in your posts. Anger. Your topics aren't exactly general interest. And, whether you like it or not, it's possible for people to link you to what you write."

He watched her face. Anger was still there, but so was a glimmer of interest.

"How'd you do it?"

"It didn't take much. I saw that 'mitandhiss' was a hosting site for a lot of protest blogs. I had to read a bunch of them until I found 'We're

81

Totally Obscene' by someone called Yavay. As you know, it was about the World Trade protests. Yavay's writing sounded like you. That was a guess; but, as it turned out, a good one, so I kept digging."

She blurted out her next question.

"What do you mean, sounded like me?"

"Back at MIT, I learned the basics of linguistic analysis—how an anonymous person can still be identified by things like word order, use of favorite words, and other internal clues. You write the way you speak. Most of us do. Those posts sounded like you."

Key looked suspicious.

"So what? You found that one thread. Big deal."

"I guessed that if you used one alias, you might use others. So I tried to figure out what 'Yavay' might mean. I worked on it with letter substitutions and arrived at 'llave'. You know, Spanish for 'key', pronounced 'yavay'. So I searched mittandhiss for 'key' in other languages, too. 'Schluss' for the German 'Schluessel', 'clay' for the French 'cle', and 'klooch', for 'klyuch' in Russian. When I found the blogs, I found your voice again."

"And you want what, brownie points for being so fuckin' smart?"

"It's not me we're talking about here. Pretty smart yourself. What made you choose foreign words as aliases?"

"My dad did crosswords. He had dictionaries. I got to thinking…"
She stopped.

"You're not going to trick anything more out of me, college boy."

Beneath the snarky comeback, he could hear she was shaken. So how would she react to the rest of what he had to tell her? Only one way to find out.

"Okay. I found you. But that's not what I wanted to show you. Look, Key, you're being followed."

She glared, balled her fists, and stomped in a tight circle. Her shouted words came out as if they'd started in a miniature blast furnace.

"Goddamn and fuck you to hell. I knew you would give away where I live. Tell me now who you told and when."

Her fists were clenched by her hips. He held up both hands, palms toward her.

"Easy. I didn't tell anyone. Yes, people broke into your house. But not because of me. When I said you were being followed, I meant there are people who follow your blogs and goad you in theirs. It could be that they're looking for you."

She took a deep breath and bowed her head for a moment.

"Yeah, some people don't like what I write. And they talk shit online. And sometimes I respond. So what?"

"You ever seen the Triplets on late-night TV?"

"You mean those losers in the commercials for Longcart Motors?"

He nodded. How could you miss them, popping up all the time, energetic, but annoying. Sometimes they wore country western clothes, guitars strapped over their shoulders. Other times they were clowns or firemen, or togged out in uniforms of the Seahawks and Mariners. They sometimes added little dance routines. But their message was irritatingly the same: Buy cars from Curt.

"So what?"

"I think they're the ones following your blogs."

She threw up her hands.

"This is bullshit."

"No. It's not. They're trying to find you. And I think they're connected to whoever ransacked your house. Here. I'll prove it."

❋ ❋ ❋

Crash swiveled back to the computer, and Key watched as his hands flitted over the keys and he opened several browser tabs at once, pulling up various websites. She stood behind him and leaned in. His reddish-blond hair was in constant motion, giving her the impression that she was reading the electronic words through an orange haze.

None of this made sense, and her gut told her to run. Just grab her bag and go. Ditch the hard drives, quit the blogging, and move somewhere far away from any of this. Eventually he paused, and the look on his face convinced her that he recognized her confusion.

"I'll try to slow down, but I want to show you how I decided it was the Triplets. Maybe then you'll believe me."

Her frustration was a seesaw, barely balanced. But she realized that if she allowed herself to sink into anger, if she ran and didn't look back, she wouldn't find out what Crash had discovered, and that could handicap her.

"Show me."

"Okay. Everyone's writing is like a fingerprint. A few words may only give you a partial. But read a lot of them, and a pattern emerges."

He pointed to a blog post in his open browser.

"You wrote this article as Klooch. Now, look at these three posts in reply. The first one uses long sentences full of grammatical errors. The next post is written by someone who likes compact blasts, ending in a zinger. This last uses the phrase 'as anyone can see' a lot."

"So?"

He switched screens, bringing up a different post.

"You wrote this one as Shluss. Different site. Different alias. Different topic. But look at the first three replies."

She scanned them. The first was written in short forceful blasts; the second was a mistake-riddled run-on sentence. Her heartbeat rose as she read the words "as anyone can see" in the first sentence of the third post.

Crash turned to look at her.

"I'd say those were written by the same people. And the same pattern is there in other posts I could show you."

She had to admit she was impressed. But not entirely convinced.

"How do I know these aren't all from you? That you're not just trying to trick me? How do I know this isn't all about payback from when I ignored you in college?"

"Key, that's stupid. I didn't know anything about your blogging before I ran into you a couple weeks ago."

"Yeah, well, doesn't matter. None of this puts me in danger if I stay offline. So I'm out of here."

She hoisted her backpack and started toward the door. Crash raised his voice and, for the first time she could remember, showed anger.

"God damn it, Key. I'm not finished. You need to hear the rest."

His reaction shocked her back to the moment.

"You have two minutes."

Crash continued.

"I've noticed that the Triplets…"

"The Triplets? Those obnoxious shits that do the used car commercials? How'd they come up in your fancy analysis?"

Crash looked up, startled. He thought a moment.

"Yeah, you're right. I should have mentioned this before. I've seen the Triplets more than I'd like to. I began to hear a pattern that stayed the same in all their commercials. It was their signature. A male makes obvious mistakes. The female replies with sarcasm. The other male, acting like a dummy, tries to sum up and almost always uses the tag line, 'as anyone can see'. When I came across these blogs, I saw the same pattern. That's why I guessed the blogs were written by the Triplets. I'd be really surprised if it isn't them."

He went on.

"One other thing. They attack you mostly when you write about logging. Have you always blogged about that?"

"No, I started about a month ago, after my father's death. I read about this new logging site, Isadka Valley. Same issues that got my dad killed. I was sad and mad, didn't think much about it, just started writing."

"The Triplet posts are too well organized to be a prank. More reason to think these people have a special purpose for reacting to your posts. And until we figure this out, you're never really going to feel safe."

Key wasn't going to respond to that. Much as she hated to admit it, Crash was making sense. The posts. The motorcycle following her. The break-ins. Walter's fall. They could be related. What if those nasty comments really were part of a plan to get at her?

Crash spoke again.

"Might as well mention something else that comes across to me. The lead writer, whoever that is, is intense. The other two not so much. They say the same things over and over, like they've been tacked on. I'm not sure what that could mean."

Neither was she, and that didn't seem important. But the idea that someone was tracking her made her let go of her backpack. She crossed her arms, looking at the ceiling.

Forget running for now. She'd stay with Crash to find out more. At least for a while.

r now. She'd stay with Crash to find out more. At least for a while.

NOVEMBER 11

Gary had gleaned basic facts about the Isadka Valley project from official reports. Reports, however, seldom contained the breath or muscle of a real-life situation. He needed that information. Most of it, he knew from his brief time in Olympia, would consist of Capitol scuttlebutt—some of it true, much of it purely imagined. You still had to use both types of information to get a complete picture.

One source was stuffed with facts but short on humanity, and the other was all too human but sometimes disregarded facts. Inwardly he laughed that a rural Indian kid—and a jock to boot—could ever put things in such terms.

That brief moment of levity was over when he realized how little forward progress he'd make unless he found a perspective that was informed but not compromised. Luckily, he knew someone who might have one.

Before he went to OPUS, he'd already started his switch from football to government work, serving for a year as a junior assistant to State Senator Miller Frederick. Jeff Winter, Frederick's chief of staff, went out of his way to help Gary get started. Over time, their relationship grew close enough that Gary got used to consulting Jeff when tough issues arose. He was back now with another one.

They sat in Jeff's cluttered cubicle at the Capitol.

"Jeff, I've been studying a logging site up north. I've got a lot of facts but I could use some advice on how to assess them. I don't want to make a mistake."

Jeff nodded. Here in the capitol he was in uniform: open-necked blue dress shirt and slacks. A tan blazer hung over the back of his desk chair, a marker that he was senior staff. Others, lower down the legislative aide ladder, raced around in khakis or jeans.

"Sounds like you're catching on. People have their little kingdoms. A turf war can easily become the main event. Important to avoid those as much as possible. I'll tell you what I can, but not too much, or I'll be obligated to tell my boss. So just give me a headline."

Gary tried to distill complexity into brevity.

"A new project is asking for permits to log near Isadka Valley. The site is similar to Gideon, where that big slide happened. So Isadka

89

Valley is getting a close look. All that's okay. But there's a chance that people who were involved in Gideon have some connection to this new proposal, and they don't want that known. For obvious reasons. OPUS will be asked for an advisory opinion soon."

Jeff crossed his arms and looked down. Gary saw a mop of blond hair turning gray, long by capitol standards but probably shorter than when Jeff had been a California surfer. It took him a while to respond.

"Now I see why you're asking for advice, and I'm glad you did. I know a little about the new project. Logging interests, eco groups, Native Americans, state regulations, and possible fraud. A couple of rungs above a trifecta."

"So what do you suggest?"

"I'll have to check further before I can suggest anything. All I can offer now is what I would probably do if I were in your shoes. But even that much is guesswork."

"I'll take anything I can get."

"Okay, I'd go to your commission and ask for more time to look into the matter, then write a report. Make it as accurate as you can, but no more. You're on a tightrope—I don't need to tell you that. On one side you could fall into reporting before your information is complete. But if you delay too much, they'll push you off the other side and replace you. So try to buy time, but always keep track of how short your rope is. Right now Isadka is a minor proposal, but it wouldn't take much, because of Gideon, to turn into a hot button, and you have to be prepared for that."

All that sounded obvious. Not really like Jeff.

"What if I don't get the extra time?"

"That's something you'll have to figure out. Maybe one of the OPUS members has particular knowledge or expertise that can help you."

Jeff looked away. His mind was on something else. He waited several beats, looked directly at Gary and went on, his words gaining speed.

"There's another thing. Could mean nothing. You need to take what I tell you as rumor at this point. On that basis, I'll tell you. Okay?"

Gary had no idea what Jeff was talking about; but he nodded anyway, and Jeff continued.

"You probably haven't heard of Grant Tomson. He's not a big or well-known player, but he's getting bigger. He prefers to operate behind boards of companies he sets up or acquires. Other people are the front men so he can stay in the shadows. Without going into details, I can assure you that Tomson is one ambitious and ruthless bastard. Right now he's laying low, because of trouble he got into concerning a lake his family owned."

"I might have heard the name."

"Well, what I have from good sources is that Tomson may have an interest in Isadka Valley. If he does, it raises both the stakes and the danger for everyone involved with that project. That's all..."

He paused.

"...except to say, be careful. I'm not sure how much Tomson has invested in Isadka, but the amount may not matter so much. Tomson can get hairy about even small amounts of money."

Gary sensed Jeff might have more to say, but he stopped. Gary thanked Jeff and left the building—still, he realized, without a specific plan.

Out in the hallway, his cell buzzed. He punched on and heard Curt Longcart's voice. No pleasantries, just a statement that sounded more like an order.

"We need to talk."

***

Laura was at the edge of the metro area and approaching Lynnwood as she drove south on I-5. She was returning in the late morning from another site visit, one well into actual logging. There she'd encountered a set of issues that seemed as simple as the ones at Isadka Valley were complicated. A thought occurred.

Two, actually. She knew Lynnwood was the location of the original showroom and headquarters of Longcart Motors. She'd never been there. But after what she had learned from Gary Seasons about Curt Longcart, it made sense for her to at least get a feel for the place.

She also might form a personal impression of the man. She'd already reported to her supervisor what she learned from Gary and the logging foreman, Rick Groff, and got an indifferent reaction. As she worked on routine tasks like the visit this morning, she kept thinking about Isadka Valley. And Longcart. He could be the key to understanding what was really going on there. His motives and involvement felt like resistance she could push on. Push hard and see what happens.

Longcart Motors was easy to find. You couldn't escape its presence in Lynnwood. As you got closer, the signs grew larger and brighter. Finally they were so overwhelming that seeing the business itself felt like an anticlimax.

Apart from the hoopla, what you had was an impressively large car lot with a sales building behind it. Used cars were the main draw. The building itself was less impressive, simple cinderblock and white paint, its basic plainness disguised by a large overhang extending from the main door. On top of it, blinking neon assaulted you with announcements of special deals.

A salesman accosted her before the car door had closed behind her. He led her to a new model Toyota, and she half listened to his pitch while her eyes scanned the display space. She spotted no one who looked vaguely like Longcart, so she broke into the sales spiel.

"Looks nice and all. I'm not looking to make a purchase today, but when I do I'll remember your advice."

The guy was about her age and trying hard. He didn't stop, just switched to talking about financing plans.

She tried a big smile.

"I'm a big fan of Curt Longcart and his commercials, especially the ones with the Triplets. I don't suppose he's around? I'd just like to say hi. Nothing else is as likely to bring me back here."

The salesman's face tried to hang on to encouragement, though a slouch in his shoulders said otherwise.

"Curt's a busy guy, but he likes to know customers. I'll see what I can do."

He disappeared through a rear door and Laura waited for several minutes. Eventually the salesman reappeared, walking two steps behind a bear of a man. He wasn't that tall; he had an immense torso to go with short legs. How those legs held up his paunch was the truly impressive part. He turned on a broad smile and immediately became the familiar TV presence she recognized. He reached out a paw.

"It's a daily pleasure to meet my friends and customers."

She quickly recorded the fringed buckskin jacket over a plaid wool shirt, both straining to cover his forward girth. Full black hair, probably dyed and ending in a youthful ponytail clashed with a weathered and lined face. His eyes, almost hidden in deep folds, told her the most. They glinted like black marbles and looked just as hard.

Laura mumbled a few words about how much it meant to her to meet him. If anything, the marbles grew harder.

"What can I tell you about our vehicles that would encourage you to upgrade to one of our specials?"

"Not today, thanks. I'm just looking, for now."

"Let's not be so hasty. Tell me more about what you're looking for so I can help you."

He had her trapped. She hadn't prepared herself for that question; and truthfully, she didn't care very much about cars. As best she could, she described an imaginary utility sports vehicle. He was now eyeing her closely.

"Sounds like you need to look at the options out front. Thank you for stopping by. What's your last name, Laura? So I can remember when you return."

She told him, reluctantly. A gotcha glint shone in his eyes. He wheeled around and lumbered back to his office. The salesman didn't bother hanging around.

She stood rooted a while before she got herself moving again. Her impulsive visit had done no good. Worse, a voice warned her. She'd probably made a mistake.

❋ ❋ ❋

Gary waited on Curt. Although earlier Curt had sounded impatient about having to schedule a face-to-face away from Lynnwood, he'd finally agreed to meet in Seattle in the late afternoon. As far as Gary could remember, this would be the first time they would have a sit-down anywhere other than in Curt's office.

The Lusty Cup, one of the trendy coffee shops that built on an anti-Starbucks cred, was the third food-related place in five years to occupy the space where he sat. It was on the west side of downtown where the city's slope dropped sharply from the eastern hills to the Sound.

Gary filled time by contemplating the light snow across the top of the Olympic Mountains. Their upper halves were visible over the tops of the older businesses that lined First Avenue. Newer buildings blocked the mountains completely.

The front door opened, and Curt stepped in. Gary watched him giving the surrounding space a careful once-over. Today Curt was dressed for Seattle in a tent-like blazer and an open-collar shirt. There was no handshake, and Curt dispensed with his usual over-the-top greeting. He plunked down in the opposite chair and stared. Gary tried to lighten things up.

"Coffee?"

"No. This won't take long."

The words were rushed, and Curt was nervous. He picked up a coaster and fiddled with it before raising his eyes.

"I got a problem, and you're going to help me make sure it goes away."

"Sure, Curt, if I can. What's up?"

"You remember the slide at Gideon? When people got killed?"

"Sure. Hard to forget."

Curt played with the coaster some more.

"What I say here goes no further, right?"

"Sure."

"Okay, seventeen individuals owned the logging parcels where the slide happened. At least that's what the permit said. But most of them were logging with money I put up. Someone who wanted to get at me could say that bundling those parcels into a larger operation went against regulations. That we got waivers we shouldn't have. That the permits were granted under false assumptions. With me so far?"

Well, well. Just what the rumors had said.

"Yeah, I follow."

Curt went on, gaining steam and sounding more like his usual overbearing self.

"You can understand, then, why the deals were done on a handshake. No paperwork. When money changed hands, it was in cash. There was a lot of scrutiny on the logging—size and location of trees, how many trees to be felled in a particular area, soil condition—that kind of thing. But there wasn't the same investigation of financing. A little sweetening to the guy in charge took care of that. That's not going to come back to bite us because the guy retired a while ago."

"So there must be another problem for you to want to talk about Gideon now."

Curt smiled, though his eyes stayed hard.

"You were always a smart kid. Yeah. There's a problem. I'll take that coffee now."

Curt looked away while they waited for his coffee to arrive. After two long sips, he spoke again.

"One of the Gideon owners got his back up. Don't remember exactly why. He had some shit idea about protecting the forest or mountainside or something. He said he might pass his complaints on. But I kinda convinced him otherwise, that there were ways I could make him and his family's lives hard if he tried anything like that. So he got in line."

"Sounds like you got what you wanted."

"Yeah, enough to go ahead and finish the project with a good profit. The parcel owners did okay, too. Even the guy who had issues, John Flanerty. But John did something I only found out about later. I met with him once along with the crew foreman, a guy named Rick Groff."

Gary made an effort this time to hide any reaction, and Curt continued, sounding more confident.

"Well, at that meeting with Flanerty, Rick heard about the real structure of the deal at Gideon for the first time. John said he was going to back out. Things got messy. Words were exchanged that could imply the deal wasn't exactly legal, and that I was threatening John."

He paused, maybe reluctant to say more.

95

"And? Did you threaten him?"

"Goddamn right I did. He wasn't just going back on his word; he was threatening the whole deal. On top of that, he spooked Rick. Later Rick wanted out, but I talked him out of it. I know he knew I could make good on my threat. I made sure Rick stayed on the job at Gideon and became the foreman at Isadka Valley."

"Sounds like you controlled everything pretty well. So what's the problem?"

Curt grimaced.

"The whole thing's getting complicated. A science group is making recommendations about slide risks. The logging companies want the recommendations to be optional. There'll be a legislative fight, and that means delay. And more scrutiny."

And now, something about Curt changed. The swagger was gone. His eyes began glancing around.

"We got the same deal going at Isadka as at Gideon, except I don't own all the markers. See, Gideon was run by one big logging company. There's a smaller one running the scene at Isadka, and I'm not sure who's really in charge. There's money groups running things now, mostly venture capitalists. All I know is that their real interest is in the small parcel provisions."

Now even a touch of fear was there—an emotion Gary had never seen in Curt before.

"What does that mean for me?"

Curt regrouped, getting some of the old menace back into his voice.

"You're going to have to deliver, sonny. Your markers are still all mine."

"What do you mean, exactly?"

"I got people keeping track. Your outfit, this Puget Commission or whatever, is doing some investigating on its own. So is Natural Resources. I'm expecting you to keep track of both of those efforts. Get my drift?"

"You want me to leak information about what's going on at OPUS and in the Department of Natural Resources? The first I can do, the second's not so easy, could be impossible."

Curt regained his full tough-guy pose.

"The word 'impossible' don't apply here. You still got your family, not to mention your career to think about, in case you've forgotten. I got people ready to swear that I never gave you help in high school and college until you pressured me hard to get it. Until you said you'd use your popularity to wreck the reputation of Longcart Motors with the tribes and hurt my bottom line. That was a big threat, what with the recession and all. Who do you think they'll believe?"

A sly smile appeared.

"If you need info, get it from that girl you've been meeting. Laura, is it?"

Gary was startled, but controlled his reaction. The only way Curt could know about Laura was if someone had been following him. He let silence be his answer and Curt went on.

"There's big money counting on everything going smoothly. One investor in particular. No telling what he'll do if things go south. Believe me, that's something for you to really worry about."

There was a missing piece. Curt was usually careful not to get in too deep in any of his slippery projects. Now he was right in the middle.

"Not like you to be in charge of all this machinery. Why?"

A different look flashed across Curt's face. Fear was there for an instant and just as quickly pushed back behind a curtain.

"I don't want you contacting me again. Remember Clif Lerman?"

Gary did. An Indian kid, maybe a couple of years younger. Came and went around Longcart Motors. Ran errands. Never talked about what he did. Both of them kept it that way.

"Yeah. And?"

"Clif still does jobs for me. You talk to him if you have anything to report, and he'll get it to me. From now on, we never had this conversation."

Gary rose and looked directly at Curt to show he got the message. No handshake, no customary ritual where Curt took Gary's hand in both of his and mumbled how he was there to help no matter what.

Back in his car, Gary sat for a few minutes, digesting the meeting. After several trips through his inner landscape, he arrived at the only point that wasn't blocked in all directions.

Curt knew about Laura Dickens. Better find out if she was doing anything more with Isadka Valley. If she was, he had to warn her. And his conversation with Jeff Winters poked in. Could the unnamed investor behind Curt be Grant Tomson? If so, he had all the more reason to tell Laura to watch her back. If Curt was scared, then the game was deadly serious.

He pulled out his cell phone and made a call.

✳ ✳ ✳

"Sure I remember."

Laura was only a little surprised at the call from Gary. It saved her the call she was about to make to him.

He went on.

"Good. Glad you do. Then you may also remember talking about small parcel exemptions for the logging permits at Isadka Valley."

"That, too."

"You and I were going to check about duplication, whether my commission and your department are working on the same issue. I don't know what you've got, but I'd like to find out. I've got something we need to discuss."

She had to be careful. An informal chat was okay; anything that implied official cooperation could get her in trouble with her bosses. Plus, football jock or not, he was a good-looking guy. Meeting him again might have a side benefit.

"Want to give me a hint?"

He hesitated.

"On a call like this, I'd rather not."

Before she could react, he went on.

"Look, when we meet I'll lay out the general idea. You can decide if I should say more. Either way, I'll make sure it doesn't get you in trouble."

Talk about vague! But, she had to admit, also intriguing.

"Okay. Let's pick a when and where. Any ideas?"

She waited through a pause.

"Actually, I've got one. I've taken up sailing. Got a small boat. I'm not much good at sailing yet, but I'm learning. Want to join me? Maybe you can teach me something."

His suggestion was so far from what she expected that she laughed.

"Any time on the water is a good time for me. But don't expect any lessons. Rowers mostly don't know much about sailors, and vice versa."

His voice relaxed.

"Don't know how well I'll manage, but there are oars for an emergency. Then you're on. Anyway, no chance we'll be overheard in the boat."

"And that matters?"

"Depends who's listening."

"There's a six-boat marina in Wallingford where Mason runs into the Ship Canal. Early morning?"

"How early's early? I'm usually out before the sun's up."

"Suits me."

They picked a day.

"See you then."

NOVEMBER 14

Key's mid-morning mood was foul, what with her cramped surroundings, and being away from her own place. It surprised her how much she missed the big house. It had almost felt like home. Most of all, she resented putting up with Crash. He'd been there when she woke up, and as soon as his work shift was done, he'd be right back there poking his nose into the middle of her business.

Her cell began buzzing. She didn't want to talk to anyone. But when she saw her Uncle George's number, she knew she had to pick up.

George lived up north, where she came from, and was almost a hermit; it took a lot to get him out of his shell. That he even had a cell phone had been a surprise to her. He was the one who broke the news to her about her dad's death, at the same time discouraging her from going to the funeral. She wouldn't have gone anyway. Her mother and siblings would have found a way to make her feel unwelcome. So she did her grieving in private.

She answered. They'd long since abandoned the ritual of greetings. George just started in.

"Had a couple of visitors said they wanted to talk to you. Said you had a tape they wanted. Didn't know what they're talking about. No problem getting rid of them, but thought you ought to know."

That was it. Message delivered. She expected George to punch off, but he cleared his throat.

"Could be you want to know they mentioned your friend Flora and that they're going to visit her next."

Then he did end the call.

Growing up, Key had lots of contact with the Indian way of life through her friendship with Flora. As kids, they were unlikely friends—she from a fractious, unpredictable Irish wild bunch, and Flora from a quiet Lummi family that exchanged words only when absolutely necessary. Key appreciated Flora's quietness, and Flora—who knows, Key never asked—might have appreciated a kind of translator in situations that must have been strange to her. Involving tough old George was one thing, Flora another. She was vulnerable in many ways.

She called Flora immediately. To her surprise, her friend picked up after the second ring.

"Flora, it's Key. I know it's been a while. I want to see you. Could we meet at the powwow? They're having one this time of year, just like usual, right?"

After a long wait, Flora spoke.

"Yeah, there's a powwow. Don't know how I'd explain to others why you're there. It's been a few years."

Flora's voice sounded brittle enough to shatter at any moment.

"Say I'll be around, visiting my family, and I gotta get away, at least for a while. The powwow would be a good break, and we can catch up."

She knew that sounded phony. When Key had moved south to Seattle, her only feelings of regret, apart from missing her dad, were about leaving Flora. For the first two years, they'd talked once a month. But the calls grew shorter, and the sense of futility in trying to have any kind of real conversation grew stronger. Eventually the calls stopped.

After another pause, Flora's voice came back on, slowed by reluctance.

"I guess it would be okay. A short visit, yeah? I'm going to ceremonies with friends."

"See you late afternoon."

So she was no longer included among Flora's friends? Or was she only hearing caution? Either way, conversation was not going to be easy.

Key called George.

"I'm coming up there today and want to borrow the old truck."

"It's gassed up."

After that, Key moved quickly. She checked the Bolt Bus schedule online and threw her few possessions into her backpack. She left Crash a note saying that she had to go back north for a day or two. Truthfully, she didn't know how long she'd be gone.

With a hand on the door knob, she looked one more time around the cramped and cluttered hole. It felt good to be getting out of Seattle and away from this place.

Just before noon she waited across the street from Union Station for the bus to arrive. Half hidden in the shadows of a deep building entrance, she would be hard for a passerby to see—just the way she liked it.

Still, there was no hiding from the memory of her earlier conversation with Crash. She remembered it word for word.

"We don't know why people are commenting on your blogs. Any ideas?"

She had pretended indifference.

"You're the one who thinks there's something suspicious going on. Just leave me out of it."

But even as she spoke, she knew that that question—that "why"—straddled the heart of her reluctance to face the past.

Going back home might help her remember more clearly the reason her father gave her the tape. She toyed with the idea that unpacking the past might be preferable to packing again for another run away.

The sight of the Bolt Bus pulling into its loading space across the street cut off those thoughts and jerked her back to the present. She climbed into the bus and found a seat. As the bus began to move, her phone buzzed. Crash.

She let it go to voice mail.

❋ ❋ ❋

Crash reluctantly punched off the call before it went to Key's voice mail. This was his second attempt to reach her. One call had been around noon. Now he was trying in mid-afternoon.

He wasn't worried, he told himself. Move on from Key's weird schedule and concerns. Just forget her. A more honest voice deeper inside dared him to try, and he knew he no longer could.

Key was doing something on her own. He'd hear from her eventually, or maybe not at all. But he didn't want to sit around waiting and worrying. He needed a task to take his mind off her.

Wherever she was, she'd be carrying with her those unanswered questions centering on her dad's death. What could he do that might help her find an answer? He let his mind rove until it settled on a pos-

105

sibility: the Triplets. Now that he'd found them online, he was curious. When in doubt, follow curiosity, his old guide.

Crash opened his computer and started searching.

The three of them had achieved considerable notoriety. He'd heard one of their tag lines, "Tell 'em Number Two," used in street conversations. KIRO News had featured them in a popular TV weekly show. An interview with them appeared in a newspaper column that sought out local characters. It was easy to learn more.

The males were twins and the female their cousin. The twins had grown up in Spokane, and the cousin in Pullman. Despite the fact that one twin, "Number Two", absorbed the brunt of skit jokes, he was also in grad school at Washington State University, studying biology. The other twin had drifted toward media jobs, as did the female cousin; and both of them lived in Seattle. The female apparently was their manager when they performed as a group.

Her real name was Suzanne Bickers and, Crash read, she worked part time with an ad agency and studied drama. She'd already filled small parts in local productions, so she probably did her part-time work in the afternoons, reserving evenings for rehearsals. He searched further and found a likely address. An apartment on lower Queen Anne Hill would offer easy public transportation to a downtown office, as well as walking distance to most of Seattle's theaters.

He'd start there.

NOVEMBER 15

Just before 9 am, Crash had a counter seat in a tiny Queen Anne coffee bar on First Avenue. Its front window faced the entrance to an older apartment building on the other side of the street. He bet that a woman would emerge who matched the pictures he'd seen online. Just after 9:15, she did.

Crash had once read a lot of showbiz bios. The woman his eyes followed was, from the neck up, Imogene Coca—short brown bob, big eyes, elfin face and all. Her lanky body could have been stolen from Carole Channing, but its movement and energy were pure Carol Burnett. He watched her turn a corner and enter a café.

The morning rush was thinning. As Crash walked past the café, he saw that the woman had a table to herself. He waited until she ordered, then entered and picked up coffee at the counter. Her head was low over a script when he walked over and pretended surprise.

"Excuse me, but aren't you one of the Triplets? I thought I recognized you."

"Yes, I am, thank you."

She was startled but not displeased. As she turned her eyes back down to the script, Crash brightened his tone.

"I don't get to meet celebrities very often. Would you mind if I joined you?"

She was cautious now, sizing him up. The smile was still on, though her gesture toward an opposite chair carried a touch of impatience.

"I suppose, but no conversation. I've got to concentrate and I'm in a hurry."

He took a sip of coffee and plunged right in.

"I actually enjoy your act and you're the best of your group, but I'm here to discuss something else, Suzanne."

That got her attention and a sharp response.

"Some nerve to ambush me like this. Whatever it is, I'm not interested. Go to my website and call my agent."

"This isn't about acting. I want to know why you've been trolling bloggers about the Isadka Valley logging project."

"I never—"

"Not even a convincing try. I know you've been doing it, and I can prove it. Some of the stuff you write verges on harassment. Threats. Twitter frowns on that, you know. I could have your face all over TMZ. The headline: small-time variety act under investigation for big threats."

His words weren't exactly defensible, but they did their job.

Her face contorted in anger. She rose and stayed that way for half a minute, blazing eyes boring into his. Then her expression changed to indecision, and she lowered herself to the chair. Crash was relieved. This tough guy act was not natural for him, and he didn't know how long he could have kept it up. She sat silent for a while, then spoke.

"I didn't want to do it. But the boys said it was okay, no big deal; and besides we needed the money."

Fear or remorse drove her words. He couldn't tell which, and decided to take it down a notch.

"You were right. Too bad they didn't listen. But the real blame goes on whoever put you up to it. Stories presenting the Triplets as character assassins could kill your careers, just when they're getting started. I'm not interested in that. I just want a name."

He held his breath. All she had to do was stand up and walk out, and he'd be nowhere. But she didn't leave. She looked up, tears welling.

"Oh, God."

He gave her a few seconds, then tried a different approach.

"Just tell me who put you up to it, and why. I'll handle the rest. And I'll leave your names out of it."

Her eyes hardened.

"Oh sure. I tell you and you'll take care of things. You've got your own game. I know nothing about you and I'm not about to trust you."

He had to regroup quickly or he'd lose her.

"I don't expect you to trust me right away. But hear me out. I'm working with a person whose life you've put in danger."

Her eyes widened, and she let out a gasp. Crash lowered his voice.

"Hey, calm down. I'm not saying you meant to do that. But you did."

She nodded and sniffed. At least she hadn't gotten up and left. Crash tried one more time.

"Suzanne, tell me who's paying you to post. If you're asked to do it again, go ahead and do it. Just let me know when it happens. In return, I keep your identities secret. Blowing your cover wouldn't give me, and the people I'm working with..."

He paused, hoping that bluff carried added weight.

"...it wouldn't give any of us an advantage. Look..."

He added what he hoped would come across as a credible sales pitch.

"...you guys, you Triplets, are very good at what you do. You're smart and funny. Who wouldn't want your humor and communication skills on their side? I'd like to free you from the pressure you're under. You're in a bad spot right now. If you play this right, you can go back to doing what you do, and making money, and no one's life will be in danger. It's win-win-win for everyone but the bad guys."

Making "win" into a triplet was a last-second inspiration that he hoped she liked. Suzanne looked away and Crash waited. She swiveled back to him.

"Rory Edwards. Don't know much about him. He works for a PR firm in Spokane now. Before that, he was an accountant. At Longcart Motors."

Crash offered his hand. She rose and shook it. Her face reflected relief.

He lowered his voice, adding what he hoped sounded like reassurance.

"We'll keep you informed. Wait. We'll need a way to stay in touch."

They exchanged numbers. Suzanne gathered her things and, without looking at him again, wheeled away and went out the door.

Crash stayed where he was. The rush he felt at having confronted Suzanne had no staying power. It leaked away fast, leaving him to figure out what really happened. First off, maybe nothing. Rory Edwards might not even be real. What was this whole blog business about, anyway? Key said it was just a hobby. But it was obviously more than that for the Triplets.

A troubling realization reared its ugly head. He still hadn't heard from Key. That's what he should be thinking about.

111

❊ ❊ ❊

In mid-afternoon, Key knocked on Uncle George's door, ninety miles north of Seattle. His matted hair and beard hadn't changed since she last saw him four years ago, though his facial wrinkles were deeper, and a slouch compressed his once straight-backed stance. He mumbled a few condolences about her dad and handed her the truck keys without asking why she wanted them. She wasn't surprised. That's what passed for communication in her family.

To kill time, she drove around aimlessly for an hour. The truck ended up taking her to a rise that overlooked a low rambling structure, her family's old house. Key looked down at the scene. It brought back none of the fabled memories of happy times that books wrote about. Within the building's walls, her mother's meanness probably still echoed. Private conversations with her father, usually in the woods, had gotten her through the teenage years.

Her dad had been away most of the time, working an 18-acre forest lot across the river from Gideon when he wasn't doing contract work for logging companies. That old lot was gone now, erased by the Gideon slide.

Her dad was gone, too, and with him the possibility of anything bearable in this place. The old house was quiet except for a couple of people coming and going. One of them, she thought, might be her mother. Not that she was about to check that out.

Fifteen minutes later, she was driving the truck west on State 20. The old transmission was making increasingly threatening noises when she saw the sign for the park.

Key knew from childhood about the powwow held in Whatcom County every autumn. Weddings, memorial services, sweat lodge ceremonies, games, eating, drinking together. Those events attracted tribes from around the region, renewed old acquaintances, and created new ones. It was a bonus that the powwow would start today, providing both a place and an excuse to meet Flora.

She was lucky to find an empty spot in a parking lot crammed with cars and RVs. Temporary booths and personal tents occupied most of the park's open space. Camping chairs, set out in clusters, filled what was left, their occupants sitting quietly or engaged in conversation. Kids ran everywhere, crackling with energy, shouting and running across a play field. Key called Flora, and they agreed to meet by the park's wooden pavilion.

Flora might once have been one of those carefree kids; Key remembered her laughter on occasions like this. But when Flora appeared, she was cautious, on guard. She stopped ten feet away. Key didn't know much about beauty, but as a girl she had thought Flora was beautiful, with soft dark eyes that hardly ever blinked, and a silky smooth face. Key remembered that face for its serenity, and for the gleaming black hair that framed it. Now deep creases emphasized down-turned lips, and lank, lusterless hair made her face look longer.

Time had also built a wall of silence. Finally, Flora breached it.

"I'm on my way to a meeting. No time to talk now. Maybe after."

Key was pretty sure there wouldn't be an "after" if she simply let Flora go.

"Can I come along, Foggy?"

Using a nickname from the past made no difference.

"Some people won't want you there. Makes no difference you still wear that bracelet I gave you."

Key glanced at the beads on her wrist. Truth was, she'd taken the bracelet for granted for so long that she'd almost forgotten where it came from.

"But most of them wouldn't mind, right?"

"Suit yourself."

Flora moved away and Key followed her.

The meeting was in a large white tent with Plexiglas windows built into its sides. A generator powered a few overhead lights and a sound system as darkness began to set in. Perhaps forty people, most of them under thirty, occupied folding chairs. She and Flora took two of them.

Up front a woman was speaking at the microphone. It took only a few sentences for Key to guess that this woman had left the reservation for the city a long time ago. Key tuned her out. The all-purpose social worker speech was exactly like the ones she heard ten years ago.

The woman finished and announced she was open to feedback and questions. Everyone was either reticent or bored. Silence made the generator's hum sound louder. Key saw movement out of the corner of her eye. A young man in jeans and a sweatshirt, two chairs over, got up and walked to the front. Slim. Mid-twenties. Black hair, slicked back. He began talking.

"My name's Clif and I'm Nez Perce. From up near Coeur d'Alene, but now here in Washington. Thought you should know about something happening out our way. No one has asked me to do this, but someone has to keep track so us Indians don't lose more just because we didn't act fast enough."

The younger people in front leaned forward. After the social worker's canned monotony, Clif's directness got attention and he built on it.

"If you don't know about the new logging project in Isadka Valley, you ought to. Some of the parcels are Indian-owned. A new project means jobs and more Indian money. It's important to all of us. Now some white politicians want to stop the project. Sounds familiar, don't it? Keep the Indians on the reservation. Don't let 'em get ahead. It's all being done behind our backs. But you can help."

Now he paused for effect, looking from face to face. He went on in a quieter, personal way.

"Help me keep this on track. Call your local representatives. Tell them this project has to go ahead."

Another pause, then a big finish.

"I'm Clif. Meet me afterwards so we can exchange email addresses and connect online. We're all in this together. I've got all this information on paper, and I'll be at the back to give it to you if you want it. It's your future. Do something about it."

He held up a bright red piece of paper, waving it high. Then he walked slowly back to his chair, making eye contact, miming a phone in one hand by his ear, the fingers on his other hand air-typing.

Key looked around. Clif got results. Cell phones and tablets were already out.

Key glanced at Flora. She was slumped, showing none of the reactions around her. The meeting ended, and the two of them shuffled with the rest of the audience toward the rear of the tent. As Key passed Clif, his eyes settled on her, and it seemed that they lingered longer than they needed to.

Outside a chill had descended, and Key knew it would turn cold fast. She half expected to have lost Flora; but when she turned, Flora was right behind her. At a fire pit, a few people held low conversations on the logs closest to the flames. A log further back was unoccupied. Key headed there, and Flora slowly did the same. They sat.

Something about the atmosphere of the powwow produced a serenity that Key vaguely recognized. There had been moments like this, years ago. She gave into the sensation enough to sit still and, as much as was possible for her, to empty her mind.

Awareness grew of Flora's presence beside her. A deep sadness filled the gap between them. Key pushed against it and in the process hunched her way closer to Flora. As kids they had bumped into each other by accident or in play, but Key could never remember them touching much on purpose. Flora stared at the fire, her arms on the log, as if she might topple without that added support.

Key reached over and laid her hand over Flora's. She felt no reaction, but Flora didn't pull her hand away either. They sat that way silently until Key offered a few words. Little by little, words became conversation. The other people left.

Their conversation was not continuous. It was more like she and Flora were putting together a catalogue of memories, separated by time and silence. It felt comfortable and right, yet sadly temporary. Flora spoke of a few fond memories, outnumbered by others that dealt with family violence and loneliness.

Would her friend be better, happier, if she came to Seattle? When a particularly long silence arrived, Key found the words.

"Flora, have you ever thought about..."

At that moment, she felt something like a hard slap, then pressure across her mouth. Before she could react, she was yanked off the log and pulled into the air.

NOVEMBER 16

Key shivered under Crash's comforter. She'd even pulled on a jacket and thrown on an extra blanket. Still she couldn't dispel the chill. Her bus ride back, and stumbling from the bus stop to Crash's place, were like episodes in a bad dream. Thoughts of the ride back led to memory of the assault by the campfire. Her mind remembered what had happened; and her legs kicked and flailed, as if she no longer controlled her own body.

Blazing anger had made no difference. All it did was keep foremost in her mind the feelings of violation and helplessness at what they'd done to her. They'd dumped her in shallow water and…Her brain locked onto that, and the shivering increased, wracking her entire body. When it subsided, she wondered for the first time whether she was going to die. She'd been in danger before, but this felt different, and she no longer had the strength to deal with it.

Where the hell was Crash? When she got back to his place, he was gone. Thank God her phone was water resistant. She'd tried at least five times to reach him. She tried again, and this time he answered.

She spoke incoherently, but Crash's reply registered.

"I'll be right there."

With that, she could relax.

And the next thing she felt was a wavelet of returning warmth coursing up the small of her back, followed by a dim consciousness of Crash's voice.

She heard herself mumbling, meant to say she was all right, then realized she was feeling…water? That woke her up. She was in a hot shower, sitting on the floor with her back against one enameled side. Steam rose around her body. Naked. Her gaze swiveled to Crash, who sat on a stool beside her.

When she'd lived in the student rental house near the U, it was pretty much impossible not to be seen without clothes at some point. One of the guys flaunted his nudity. She didn't care. Neither had she cared in her family growing up, where clothes were often optional.

She felt no danger from Crash. His eyes stayed on her face, and they reflected only concern. But his eagerness to help created an unexpected problem. Her usual aggressive attitude felt out of place, and

119

that made her feel naked in a different way. She didn't know what to do or say, and she felt...God, she hated this new feeling, and hated even worse giving it a name: She felt shy.

Crash asked about eating. Then he turned off the water and helped her stand. He dried her back and legs, while she dabbed at places she could reach and still stay upright. Hazily she got into a pair of sweats. Vaguely she realized they were in the big building beside Crash's shack. He helped her out a hall door, across an outside storage yard, and into his place.

Inside, he draped a blanket over her shoulders and half-led, half-carried her to the big chair. A mug of soup appeared in her cupped hands. After the first swallow, she could hold the mug without assistance.

He waited until she finished the soup.

"Can you tell me what happened?"

Yes, she could, but she didn't want to relive it. Not now. He waited until she felt strong enough to try. She spoke brokenly; small shivers came and went.

"I was sitting with my friend Flora by a campfire and some guys grabbed us...took us into the woods...water...held me down...beat up Flora...told me to leave, I shouldn't be there...told me next time I'd die. Dumped me in the water and left."

The thoughts brought with them a huge tremor.

Crash's lips squeezed down, forming a straight line under blazing eyes. She'd never seen that look on him before, almost didn't recognize him. Words came out slowly, like it was hard for him.

"Don't bother with more now. You need to eat, if you can. Then sleep."

She could do that. She should also put him back where he belonged, back in his own life, so she could run her own. So she could run away as soon as she decided to. But she was too weak for that, and a strange feeling stood in the way.

She didn't want to be alone. And it wasn't just that. Maybe she needed help to make it at all. Maybe if she ran she'd still need help.

She started to doze and felt herself being lifted, then lowered. Her hand brushed a rough surface, and she knew she was on a mattress. Then she slept.

❋ ❋ ❋

Gary was aware that Laura was watching him. He could see the expression on her face now. Gray dawn was gradually turning into early morning. Fog still hung in patches across Lake Union's surface.

Laura looked out across the lake, but he felt her eyes return to him, and he caught an amused expression on her face.

Though he'd grown up around coastal Lummis, his blood was mountain Salish, inland along the Skagit River—hunters, mainly. Anyway, the Lummis were canoers, not sailors.

The Bug was only a ten-footer, just able to accommodate two people, but better for a single sailor. He'd bought the boat to learn in, not to accommodate others. Its molded polyethylene hull was light and tough, and the boat had oars, along with an outboard mounting. If his technique improved, he could upgrade to a performance mast and larger sail.

Laura must have been reading his mind.

"You need a bigger boat."

"Yeah, eventually. When I know the ropes. I learned my lesson when I went out past the locks and ran into weather in the Sound. Had to go to the motor. The Coast Guard came alongside. Said next time they'd have to cite me."

"I can see why. But I guess you're having fun."

"Fun's okay. I was looking for relaxation, too. I'll have to wait on that until I'm farther up the learning curve."

The boat was moving, but their conversation was treading water.

Laura helped him.

"So you're another jock, like me. Tell me how you got into politics. I can't help being curious."

He bought time adjusting the rope in his hand. The adjustment did nothing, and he still felt awkward.

"I guess you'd have to say I drifted in. Division 1 football really cuts into study time. So I chose a major in ecology because I grew up in a rural area. I thought the subjects would be easy, and they were anything but. Only got to a few of the advanced courses, but I kinda liked it."

"And then?"

"After the Seahawks cut me, I worked for a couple of years in their front office in PR. It was boring, and they weren't getting much outta me. But, on the side, I got an environmental tech degree at Bellevue College, then a degree in general studies at the U. *The Seattle Times* found out, did a story on that. I got a call about a job at the legislature. I didn't know anything about politics. Lesson one was learning that a state senator would think my heritage was worth showcasing. And even if that's how I got the job, I'm making damn sure I do it as well as I can."

He heard the defensiveness in his voice. If Laura heard it too, she didn't let on. Instead she laughed.

"I know that song. Two drifters off to see the world. Just not the world we expected. But as long as we're talking, maybe you can help me. I'm getting better at the technical part of my job, you know—absorbing facts, deciphering reports, that kind of thing—but I need more. I want to do a job well, but also have more than a job, if you know what I mean?"

He nodded. Sure he did.

She looked back toward the docks.

"Maybe it's different for you. I'm guessing you're not as unmoored as I am. You were brought up in an area where logging once was the major industry. It influenced everything in peoples' lives. You're also an Indian, and I assume that comes with its own cultural view. So what does our work mean to you?"

Gary understood exactly what Laura was asking. But he hadn't expected the question. He knew she didn't mean it that way, but he felt temporarily like a fourth grader again, an Indian kid answering a question in front of a sea of eyes, all assessing him, judging him.

Elsewhere he could have absented himself for a moment, gotten away from that image. But there was no escape from it in a small boat. He did have something to say about purpose and passion. He'd thought about those things, just never said anything about them out loud. He tried now, and heard himself fall back on predictable remarks. He sounded to himself like a cross between a freshman parroting an ecology text and a tribal PR man making hackneyed statements about the sacred connections between Native Americans and their ancestral lands.

Gary could see he was disappointing her, so he stopped. He felt embarrassed. He needed to recoup. There had been a reason for holding this conversation on a boat. He brought it up now, before another long silence could wipe out conversation altogether.

"No one can listen in here."

She leaned toward him so their words wouldn't be lost in the wind. "About what?"

"Curt Longcart. He helped me out when I was in high school and later at the U. I tried to be careful about accepting outside money that would be illegal. What I didn't know was that he was also giving my family money, and asked them not to tell me. So I may, technically, have violated NCAA rules. Or, at least, it could be presented that way, if someone wanted to."

"I get that, but what would be the harm now?"

"Worst case, the NCAA could still sanction the U. They might have to forfeit games they won while I was playing. That could cost them big bucks, and I'd be blamed. It could also make me unemployable. I don't like that, but I could handle it. But there'd also be blowback against my family. And Indians in general. For that, I don't want to be responsible."

"Still, someone would have to point to the violation. Who would do that? Does Longcart have a reason for revealing your old arrangement?"

"Yeah, possibly. It involves Isadka Valley."

She leaned away, while one hand moved up and down the gunwale, seeking a grip. Then shifted back.

123

"Okay. But why now, and why are you involving me?"

"I haven't involved you yet. Why now? Because Longcart was one of the silent partners at Gideon, and he's doing the same thing at Isadka. And there may be another partner, a guy named Grant Tomson, who's putting pressure on Longcart."

"What kind of pressure?"

"I don't know. But I do know what Longcart is most worried about: a conversation that was taped, a while back, that lays out the real workings at Gideon. The tape's still out there, and someone, maybe Tomson, wants it. I think Tomson could be leaning on Curt, and that makes Curt nervous. There's a lot of money on the line. Curt wants me to report anything I find out."

She fired right back at him.

"Are you going to ask me to be one of your spies?"

Damn it. He'd handled that wrong.

"No. You don't know me, but I'd never do that. All I'm asking for is advice, if you have any to offer."

"Me, advice? I'm newer at all this than you are."

She was right. This was a bad idea. Gary returned his attention to sailing, and Laura seemed to be somewhere else, maybe wishing she was on dry land. A few minutes later she surprised him.

"I was pretty harsh. You took me by surprise. The advice part is reasonable. I just can't think of anything useful."

She laid her hand on his shoulder as she spoke. He liked the feel of that. She might have seen his smile.

Her hand stayed on his shoulder only a second or two before she returned it to her lap.

"Well, I'm finished. What do you say we head back?"

He nodded, and soon they were on a course back to the dock. Her next words were more encouraging.

"No hurry, though. Given a choice of being on water or anywhere else, water wins. Besides, you're doing better, even if you need more practice."

"I hope you'll come along to help when I do it."

She showed the hint of a smile but said nothing about the implied invitation. He hoped that was not a subtle "no". From the start, he had felt that Laura was one of the rare women he might relax with. He still thought so, despite the way he'd botched things.

Once they were on the dock, she hesitated.

"I haven't forgotten about Longcart. If I think of something, I'll let you know."

"Good. But before you actually do anything, you maybe should check with me. Longcart's more dangerous than he lets on. He also knows that Natural Resources is taking a close look at Isadka."

Should he also say that Curt knew that he and Laura were working together? No, not for now. She was unlikely to seek out Curt without her boss's permission. Why complicate things?

"Thanks, I'll keep that in mind."

She moved away and flicked a "See ya" over her shoulder.

He hoped his last words had registered.

❋ ❋ ❋

Crash stood up from the lounger and did stretches for his back, shoulders, and hamstrings. By now, early dawn showed outside his window. Sitting too long tightened everything, and his muscles had decided to fight each other out of boredom.

When he'd done enough to loosen up, he carefully opened the door and looked in on Key. She was asleep, this time without frequent jerks. He closed the door, went to the small fridge, and ate a few bites of leftovers. Judging from the aftertaste, it must have been cheese and pepperoni. He added a cup of instant coffee.

Now he was wide awake. Anger and urgency ran through him like a triple espresso. During one of her periods of wakefulness last night, Key had started talking. He'd gone into the room where she was sleeping. She rambled, dozed, rambled again.

"...just sitting there and they grabbed me...yelled in my ear that I didn't belong...powwow was for Indians...teach Flora a lesson she'd never forget... beating her...then in the water...held me down, all but my head… really cold…shaking…stayed there…sure they were gone…"

He seethed as he imagined her being attacked—tossed around, threatened, and left in a ditch on a near-freezing night. The thought of her helplessness had made him want to yell, and he was glad that a stronger internal voice reminded him of the need to keep her calm.

"Why'd they do it? Were they drunk?"

"…not that drunk…one guy kept looking into the woods…like there was someone else back there…"

"Did you ever see him?"

"…no…but I can guess…"

"Who?"

"… heard one say 'Clif'."

"Clif?"

"Spoke earlier…said he was Indian…"

"Forget that for now. Tell me what happened next."

Her words slowed, and she started speaking more clearly.

"Flora and me walked back, holding each other up. She was hurt and I was so cold. It was quiet when we got to our cars. She wanted to go home and drove off in her car. I barely made it to my uncle's place. He wanted me to stay. I said no and he drove me to the bus station. I was shivering all the way. Don't remember much except finally getting here and trying to call you."

He'd felt a terrible dread. When he finally let out his breath, he realized how long he'd been holding it.

"I wish I could have been there to protect you."

In the light that filtered through a high window, he thought he saw her eyes fill with resignation and sadness.

"I'm used to it."

Those simple words contained an ocean of meaning. Too much for them to explore. He waited until she dozed off again, then lay beside her for a long time with his eyes wide open until he got up and moved to the lounger.

Now he thought about what to do. Yesterday he'd suggested calling the police, but Key was alert enough to say no. Anyway, it was not for him to report to the police or anyone else. But he might be able to get information that would help Key make the decisions only she could make.

He should follow up on what Suzanne Bickers had revealed.

He had a little time before he was due at the glass studio, so he went to the computer and read articles on Isadka Valley. Narrowing his focus to early mentions of the project, he found a single article on a business site that mentioned possible investors in a logging project there.

He recognized one name: Grant Tomson, the guy who'd made headlines a while ago at Tomson Lake. What was the problem? Oh yes: Who actually owned the property, Indian tribes or the Tomson family? Crash was intrigued that Tomson was referred to as a "prominent" local businessman, and yet for sure he had not heard or read anything about the man for over a year.

What could a "prominent" businessman who had disappeared from the news have to do with Isadka Valley? That question would never have occurred three weeks ago. But now Isadka might be entwined with Key's history and even with her safety. Curiosity might have pushed him to follow up, but he knew that there was more; concern was in the driver's seat now.

Making sure that Key was comfortable, Crash left her a note and decided to walk to the glass studio on a detour that would take him by Tomson's office in South Lake Union. The office occupied a sliver of a building that wouldn't stay standing much longer; big construction cranes were already nearby. Crash checked the address. It jibed, even if there was no identifying sign by the entry. A guy who might be an employee on break leaned against the bricks as he smoked.

As long as he was here…

"Is this where I'll find Grant Tomson?"

The man didn't move, though he showed surprise.

"Who's asking?"

Crash improvised.

"A potential investor. Likely to make an appointment later."

The man straightened and looked him over. Crash realized the impression he made: jeans and a pullover on a short guy, hair overdue for a cut, and a mid-twenties face. The guard didn't bother to hide his skepticism, even contempt.

"Mr. Tomson would need to see your resume before even considering a meeting."

"Understood. But I've got a schedule, too. Can you tell me when he'll be back?"

Uncertainty flickered across the man's face. Then a hard, final look pushed it away. The conversation was over.

The guy resumed his former position. Crash could feel eyes tracking him as he walked away. Big deal. So stopping here was useless. Chalk up one more on the minus side. No harm done.

He turned back north, lengthening his stride so he wouldn't be late for work.

❊ ❊ ❊

Grant Tomson looked down at his knees. They were shaking. He'd been angry before, but never like this.

Within the last hour he'd gotten four calls, each giving him another part of the same news. Those idiots. It could all be different if any of them had called earlier.

Curt told him about some woman stopping by, posing as a customer and doing a bad job of it. At least he'd gotten her name. Laura Dickens had a social media presence, including LinkedIn. A rower, now at Natural Resources. Not likely to be a coincidence.

Clif Lerman reported that he'd actually had the Flanerty girl under his control and didn't realize what she was worth. After years of looking for the tape, its owner had slipped through his fingers.

Third, a stranger was asking for him at his offices. Could have been a nobody, or a reporter trying to look inconspicuous. But Grant Tomson didn't believe in coincidences.

At least his other contact had called to report that Flanerty had been quiet on her blogs. That was good. Maybe the roughing up she got on the net would stop her incessant writing about Isadka Valley.

128

Still he didn't like the messiness of it all. Too many sous chefs cooking up lousy results. His best—his only—choice was to take charge personally. Besides, that's exactly what he wanted— no, needed— right now. Those incompetent idiots would find out who he really was.

He made three calls and gave explicit orders. Each listener, on command, repeated word for word what he said.

NOVEMBER 17

Key awoke. Confusion and terror had shrunk to a hazy dream. Gone was the sense of immediate danger that woke her the last two nights. Crash, too, was gone, but she found a large paper cup from a local coffee shop, a bran muffin, a protein bar, and a note saying he'd be back soon. It ended with "Please don't leave."

She ate, showered, and put on fresh clothes. Those essentials done, memories of the powwow began to intrude again. She made an effort to shift her thoughts to Flora. She shouldn't have left her friend so unprotected. Key picked up her phone.

A voice she hardly recognized answered.

"Flora, it's Key. How are you?"

"What I expected."

Key had to strain to make out the words. Flora sounded as if she couldn't convince her lungs to deliver enough air.

"You okay?"

Anger increased the volume slightly.

"As if you care."

Key wanted to do something, anything. A half-born thought turned into words before she'd fully formed it.

"Look, why don't you come to Seattle? I've got room. A safe place."

Silence.

"C'mon, Flora, why not? I saw what happened to you. You're not just a friend, you're the only friend I've ever had, and I've been out of touch way too long. I want to talk. About a lot of things. We can't talk up there where you are. You'll be in danger if I'm around."

She was beginning to think that prolonged silence was the only answer she'd get, when Flora surprised her.

"When?"

Reality paid an overdue visit. Now she was stuck with a promise and no plan. The big house was still a dangerous place to stay.

"Not right now. There are a few things to get ready. Then I'll call and we'll make arrangements. I promise."

A shorter silence, then she heard the same fragile voice that first answered.

"Like I'll ever hear from you again."

The phone went dead.

Key sank into the lounger as reactions washed over her. She felt unaccustomed relief and embarrassment, and burst into tears. Good thing no one else was around. She never cried. She waited until her sobs subsided, then thought again about what to do. She couldn't stay here forever, and she didn't want to. She wanted her own place. Her own safe place. The big house was the only one she'd ever known—for a while, anyway.

She hated to admit it, but she missed that place. But they couldn't go back until they found out who was after her.

She caught herself using the plural "they". She wasn't with Crash because she wanted to hook up with him, only because she had no other option. As soon as she did, she'd split. In the meantime, this was a place to stay, even if it felt forced on her by circumstances; and Crash had resources, like his computers.

She heard Crash returning. He brightened when he saw her in the chair.

"You look a lot better."

She tried a smile, not really sure how it looked.

"Maybe on the outside, but there's a lot more to do."

"Yeah, I know. I've got my own list. What's on yours?"

"Find out who broke into Walt's house to get the tape, and who's behind them. That's at the top."

"My number one, too."

"And I've complicated things. I invited Flora to come here. Can't do that until the house is safe."

"Calling the police won't do much. Just draw attention to you living there."

"That's for sure. And it might cause trouble with AlkiSteel. More hassle we don't need."

He nodded.

"Tell me more about that tape."

"I only heard it once and can't remember much."

"Why'd your father record it?"

"He was a logging foreman and a land owner, and was being asked to do something he didn't want to do. Something illegal. I think the bastards killed my dad because he could expose something at Gideon. He was just a small parcel owner, but the other owners had big money behind them. And I think they could be the same people running Isadka Valley. They took away the only person in my life who treated me decent. My mom? She didn't, and still doesn't, give a shit. My dad liked that I was smart. I think that's why he gave me the tape and didn't even tell the others about it."

She was surprised to hear herself blurt out so much. She glanced at Crash, but he didn't seem fazed. His reply matched his calm expression.

"I'm sorry that was your life then. Let's see what we can do about making it better now. A start would be to listen to that tape."

She read a question on his face, and his next remark confirmed it.

"Of course, we have to get to the tape first. I'm guessing you hid it before we left your place."

She hesitated, immediately on guard. Did he really want to help? Or had he planned this clever way to box her in? She was about to reply when a familiar inner voice shouted: Don't trust anyone.

NOVEMBER 18

"You did ask me to keep you informed. Isn't that what you wanted?"

Gary pictured Jeff Winter listening on the phone at his cluttered desk in Olympia, and could hear hesitation in his response.

"Yeah, absolutely. But the Laura Dickens part worries me. Talking to her on a personal level, for a heads-up, is okay. Those kinds of conversations go on all the time. But did she promise not to give her bosses your information about Longcart and Tomson? Not yet anyway?"

"Not in so many words, but we agreed that neither of us should take it any higher until we have a better handle on what's really going on."

"Just be sure you keep it that way as long as you can. There may be a time soon when you can't. If that happens, report up the line right away and let me know. Any delay will mean trouble for you, one way or another."

Gary couldn't help letting out a small laugh. The irony got to him.

"I got it. I'm inexperienced enough that I need advice from my boss, but I shouldn't talk to my boss until the moment's right. Nice advice."

Jeff added his own laugh.

"Welcome to the club. You can still talk to me."

"Okay, then, I'll take you up on that right now. Longcart implied that Grant Tomson has a stake in Isadka Valley. You told me before, Tomson is a businessman, likes to work behind the scenes. Anything more I should know?"

Gary heard a grunt.

"Unfortunately, yes."

"Unfortunately?"

"There's a lot I can say on the subject of Grant Tomson. Some of it's personal for me. I don't want to tangle you in my past, but this much is important: in addition to being smart, Tomson's ruthless. He'll do just about anything—anything—to win. He's well-connected, and if you mess with one of his deals, you should assume that one way or another he'll go after you. Best bet is always to figure he's closer than you think."

"Okay. So should I stay away from Tomson completely? What if I get closer to him without meaning to? Or learn something important about him? Do you want me to keep you informed about that?"

"Yeah, absolutely. There are a couple of people on the east side of the mountains who also should know if anything bad happens. I'll take care of them. And…I guess this is as good a time as any to give you this contact."

Gary heard papers rustling.

"What for?"

"Best to be prepared. Tomson moves fast, and you never know when you might need help…Here it is, the office number. I'll give you his cell, too. It's for a policeman in Swiftwater…"

"The town just past Snoqualmie summit?"

"Right. But Bill McHugh…"

"McHugh? I think I know that name. Part Indian? Yakama, if I remember right. Got involved in a rescue in the mountains a couple of years back. Made the papers over here."

"That's him. Anyway, he knows more about Grant Tomson than I do. Still wants Tomson for another crime. If you need help from the police with Tomson, McHugh won't be able to provide direct assistance outside his jurisdiction. But he's well connected and could get other jurisdictions to help, if necessary. Like I said, Tomson's a dangerous guy."

❋ ❋ ❋

Laura finished reading two environmental impact statements. One dealt with the demolition of a viaduct along the Sound in downtown Seattle. The tunnel project to bypass I-5 was getting back on track, and competing plans for remaking the waterfront were vying for attention. The second study was still in preliminary stages: a project that would merge bus and light rail systems. Although implementation was years away, residents of Mercer Island were already taking a stand against the project's impact on their community.

She worked efficiently and decided to use a few minutes of her saved time to look at something entirely different.

Gary had mentioned Grant Tomson. Laura already knew something about him, but not enough. When she was working with an outdoor recreation project in the mountains near Swiftwater, her boss, Sara Winter, had negotiated to use the Tomson family's lake property and had gotten personally involved with Grant. The project had not gone well, and, toward the end, Grant may or may not have assaulted Sara. It was her word against his.

Now Tomson's name was possibly linked to Isadka Valley. She searched for Tomson online and found lots of news items and press releases up to a year ago, but nothing after then. It was as if Tomson disappeared.

Going back five years, you couldn't miss him. He was an investor/ developer who wanted to be known, and he succeeded. Publicity assistants must have worked overtime. One of his acquisitions even made the business page of the New York Times. He was often mentioned in stories about social and fundraising events. He'd been married and divorced twice, and afterwards appeared in photos with different gorgeous females on his arm. He had a way of positioning himself as a crucial final supporter of many projects.

The hyperactive social side of Tomson had a parallel in the extreme physical fitness side. He entered distance races and hung out with advocates of an ultra-fitness exercise regime called The Winners. She knew both the benefits and dangers of ultra-exercise. There was something compulsive about the way Tomson kept in shape. As if his real competition was not with others, but with aging.

Laura thought about what she'd read. She doubted that Tomson had changed. Most likely he was still the same aggressive money man, working his way up the pecking order to power—super-confident, and narcissistic. He clearly liked publicity, so what could possibly keep him out of the public eye for so long?

Maybe he needed secrecy because attention would mean scrutiny. And if he didn't want scrutiny, whatever he was involved in must be valuable or vulnerable in some way. If Isadka Valley was the venture in question, then her simple task—analyzing requests for logging permits— could prove to be far from routine.

141

She and Gary Seasons were continuing to analyze Isadka. That part was on schedule and faced no major hold-ups. Gary suspected, from what Longcart had said, that Tomson might be involved. But Gary's hands were tied because of his history with Longcart. She couldn't take any of this to her boss; it was too vague. And no one at Natural Resources would want to investigate an influential businessman—that person's job, even the agency's budget, could be put in jeopardy.

Hadn't she been looking for a purpose? Something beyond shuffling paper and reading about viaducts? Tomson was dangerous only if she did something to provoke him. Up to that point, any information she could bring into the mix could be helpful.

One possibility occurred: focus on Longcart. That might bring Tomson out of his hole.

Her old push-ahead default was taking hold. It always carried some risk. But for now, there didn't seem to be a downside. Besides, the rush of anticipation at doing more than reading and commenting on reports really felt good.

NOVEMBER 21

"Take it easy. I'm sure Suzanne's running late."

Crash didn't know for sure. But he wanted to keep the storm warning on Key's face from building into a hurricane.

He'd brought her along to the glass studio. They sat side by side at his favorite spot, at the longest table in the world. He didn't know of any official listing, but figured it was doubtful that any other table could beat this one. It had been cut as a single piece from the center of a Douglas fir, and stretched over a hundred and forty feet, end to end. Windows that stretched the length of the table gave them an unobstructed view of Lake Union.

This had been the U's original boathouse, and held a special place in the US history of rowing. The radical scull that brought home an Olympic gold medal in 1936 had once held an honored place in its long-gone racks. Crash had permission to relax and eat meals here. He much preferred it to the fevered working areas where teams of glass blowers were sweating their art.

The last five days had gone by slowly. Key needed time to recover. He felt a sad delight in taking care of her, but he couldn't deny the selfish pleasure of finally being close, bringing her food, taking her on short walks around the neighborhood, staying beside her at night until she fell asleep. Now she was back to normal, wearing her familiar scowl of impatience.

He'd brought her along to meet Suzanne, though he had no idea how Key would react to meeting one of her harassers. In attitude and speech, Key and Suzanne could not have been more different. Oil and water? No. More like TNT and nitro. At least, that's the way it felt, once he faced the actuality of having both of them at the same table.

Two minutes more and Suzanne arrived. Her hair was auburn today. He guessed she might dye it often. Nothing could change her gangly frame and gamin face, though. She toned down the affected gestures she had brought to their first meeting. Good thing. Otherwise, Key would be the first to start the insults.

He gave Suzanne a minute to gush about how thrilled she was to be in the famous glass artist's studio, then got down to business.

145

"Thanks for coming. I took my lunch break early so we could talk. But just to make sure we're all at the same starting point. Suzanne…"

He looked at her.

"…you told me, and I've told Key, about how someone pointed you toward Key's blog posts and paid you to harass her online. Now, let's talk about how the Triplets can make up for that lapse in judgment."

Without missing a beat, Suzanne pushed back.

"Lapse in judgement? All we did was question those posts, and put the issues in a different light. Blogs are mostly innuendo anyway, not exactly investigative journalism."

Key snorted, but Suzanne went on.

"Look, we made some lame threats, but they meant nothing. We did nothing illegal. And it wasn't personal. We did it because we needed the money. Have you ever tried to make a living in the arts? Choices are never pure. Sometimes you just do what you gotta do."

Crash put his palms up.

"Bad choice of words. But let's talk about what to do now."

Before their meeting with Suzanne, Crash had tried out an idea on Key. If their purpose was to find out who was behind the attempt to get Key's tape, and if part of that attempt included the Triplet's blogs, then it made no sense to stop the Triplets from blogging. Better to keep them going, and also get them to generate other conversations involving more people. His reasoning was that larger public interest in the logging issues that Key was raising might increase their chances of finding out who was after her. If a persistent voice emerged, they could investigate. If no individual stood out, generating public interest in sites like Isadka was still a plus.

Oh, come on. All that was vague. Face it, his real focus wasn't blogging or Isadka. It was Key, keeping her safe and extending the possibility that she'd let him be a part of her life. He was grasping at what was available. At least those ideas helped convince Key to meet with Suzanne.

Suzanne sighed and took a deep breath.

"Okay."

Crash was no surer where to take things but jumped onward anyway, from rock to rock over the conversational swamp. Teetering for balance at each landing. Two gators circled, named Key and Suzanne.

"To start with, we want to get at the guys who used you. One starting point is Rory Edwards, the guy you told me has been passing orders on to you. Who's controlling him? You can help us find out."

Yesterday, Crash had researched old business directories. Before his current job as an accountant in a PR firm in Spokane, Edwards was listed in the "About Us" web page of Longcart Motors.

"And how do I do that?"

Crash saw Suzanne steal a glance at Key, who was staring down at the floor.

"Here's an idea. If Edwards gives you other assignments, go ahead and accept them. Write what he wants and—here's what's new—write other things that Key will suggest."

A tidbit from some showbiz careers that he'd read about inspired him out of the blue.

"You can even develop a whole new threesome of personas. Give the Triplets a boost in the process."

Expressions came and went across Suzanne's face: suspicion, then perplexity. She stood, as if intending to leave. Instead she did a couple of stretches and sat again. Crash caught a glimpse of interest, then a look of calculation that stayed put.

Suzanne glanced at Key, but directed her question to Crash.

"What if she doesn't want to work with us?"

That was it for Key. She fired back.

"You want to say something, say it to me."

Crash was all set for Suzanne to wilt. But she surprised him, looking directly at Key.

"Actually, I do have something to say, now that I have your attention. I'll go along with this—write some bullshit posts or tweet about logging or whatever. But trust me to figure out how to get the message out. You know the content, and you've got access to all the sites, but I know more about style than you do. We're either partners in this, or nothing happens."

Key lowered her gaze and mumbled.

Suzanne laughed.

"Not sure what you said. I don't hear that well."

Key looked up, her glower intact.

"Not convinced yet. But keep talking. Just as long as we find out who's behind all this."

Crash exhaled.

"Now that that's settled, let's talk specifics."

For the next ten minutes they did. After that, Crash had to get back to work. Key and Suzanne barely looked up when he stood. They were still talking when he took one last glance at them. Both appeared wary but no longer angry. This was good.

But Key also didn't notice his departure even enough to say goodbye.

❄ ❄ ❄

Key stopped outside in front of the glass studio. Suzanne had gone out first and stood beyond, talking on her cell phone.

By the side of the studio, a high hedge grew in front of a lower chain-link fence. A gap in the hedge revealed a sliver of Lake Union. Key walked over to it and followed the view down to the south end where she could pick out buildings, but not details. Her own situation was the opposite: She could give details but hadn't yet arrived at any general perspective.

Blogging didn't count for much—for sure, not enough to change public opinion on a big issue like logging. So she could take blogging or leave it. She'd gotten into it by accident, anyway. Surfing the web in her lonely downtime after moving to Seattle, she'd run into a post that was angry about logging and seemed directed at people like her father. She wrote an angry reply. That felt good, so she looked for other negative posts about logging. Later she found posts insulting Indians, dismissive about people like Flora. She wrote angry replies to those, too, eventually writing full posts herself, and not just about logging—about politics and corruption and the social issues that Walt cared about.

148

After her father's death, she'd doubled down on the blogging, which is when she'd started to attract more replies—nasty comments she now knew were the work of Suzanne. All that activity had helped in the moment, but the more she shed her grief, the less she cared about the blogs. Then Crash discovered them and they seemed important again, because no one should mess with what was hers. Now she didn't care much anymore. So why not just walk away from everything?

On the other hand, maybe continuing would help small loggers and the tribes who often got shafted by bigger interests. Her dad had been one of those small loggers. Flora was Indian. Any leverage against the big interests was a plus for people like them. For others, too. Sure, a single blog post would never swing public opinion, but maybe something that hit harder, like Suzanne suggested, could make a difference.

She wasn't finished with those thoughts when she felt a tap on her shoulder and turned to find Suzanne close behind her.

"You know, I didn't look forward to this meeting. I thought you guys were going to threaten me and try to force me into something. But you didn't. And talking to you helped me understand a few things. Thank you."

Key offered a neutral nod in return.

Suzanne went on.

"I've got some ideas for blog posts. But there's more to do. Long-cart counts on support of the tribes. One thought occurred. Gary Seasons—you know, "Chief Hawk"—used to work for Curt and knows a lot about his business. But Curt must have had some kind of falling out with him—Chief Hawk doesn't come around anymore, and I've heard Curt talking shit about him. If they're on the outs, maybe Seasons would want to help us out with our new messages. Just a thought. Bye for now. Gotta run."

Key waited for Suzanne to flounce around the corner of the parking lot, then waited longer to make sure she was really gone.

She needed to regroup. Go back to Crash's place? That was a safe haven. But maybe she didn't need it anymore. Everything she'd brought to Crash's was in her knapsack. Except the tape, of course. So she didn't have to go back.

The big house? Funny how it kept popping up in her mind. Running meant starting over completely, and she really didn't want to do that again. Maybe it was time to stand her ground—get to the bottom of who was after her so she could be free.

As she stared out across the lake, the big house beckoned her. But she couldn't go back—not just yet. She would need better security first. The thought of that felt good. How could she make it happen? She needed to talk to Jim Purgis, Walt's ally at AlkiSteel, the guy in charge of plant maintenance.

She called Purgis. He agreed to get together and raised no objection when she asked to see him away from the plant. They agreed to meet at Salty's Restaurant in Alki.

Two hours later, after the lunch rush was over, they faced each other at a table on the water side. Through the window beside them, they had a postcard view of the Seattle skyline. Purgis glanced around the mostly empty dining area and spoke first.

"First of all, I'm sorry you lost Walt."

Washed-out blue eyes regarded her from a wrinkle-free pink face topped with a thinning white buzz cut. Beefy hands, clasped on the table, showed the age and damage that the face hid.

"You too."

She waited. He shifted forward.

"On the phone, you mentioned a break-in."

"Yes, and I'd like to find out what can be done about better security."

"A lot of things. Walt never put in any deterrents. But there's something else I need to tell you first."

"Go ahead."

"I know you're getting the house. Walt told me. While Walt was living, continuing maintenance on the plant's dime was a kind of thank-you to him. Everyone up the line agreed we should do that as long as he was alive. A few weeks ago—you don't know this because no public announcement's been made yet—AlkiSteel got bought out by a German multinational. There was verbal agreement that maintenance of Walt's house could go on as long as he lived, but no longer. I was in some of those discussions and could tell our new bosses didn't like giving even that much. You get what I mean?"

"That you can't do anything about the house security."

Purgis glowered, then smiled.

"Can see why you think that. But I'm still a senior VP, and with me a handshake deal with Walt takes precedence over a deal with the Krauts. Until I get a direct order to do otherwise, anyway. So we'll fix any damage from the break-in, put in a security system, and link it to cell phones so our watchmen know when it goes off. And we'll add your house to the night rounds. But I gotta warn you that pretty soon all the plant's help will stop. Gas and water will be cut off, and you'll be..."

He thought for a moment.

"I was about to say on your own. But as long as I'm there, I'll see if I can get around our Teutonic masters. Trouble is, I plan to retire in February. That's your window."

Key thanked Purgis. They discussed a few details and hurriedly finished their coffee. He left, and she sat at the table a little longer. Her eyes were pointed at the view, but her thoughts were on Flora. With security in place, there would be no reason for her not to come to Seattle. Flora would be safe, and she, Key, could get back to her old life. Maybe a better one.

She caught herself. There were problems. But one by one, she was taking care of them, and an end was in sight. Crash was a problem only if she let him be.

She knew her next move: Leave Crash's place and get back to Walt's old house. Her house. It felt good to call it that.

NOVEMBER 23

"Yeah, I know who you are."

The voice on the phone came out like a growl. Jeff Winter had given Gary the number for Bill McHugh, the policeman in Swiftwater, to be used in case of an emergency. No emergency yet. But if football had taught him anything, it was about anticipation and preparation. An emergency was no time to make first contact.

"Sounds like I got you at a bad time. Sorry. I'll try again later."

"Hold on. You said Jeff Winter gave you my number?"

A pause.

"Okay. At least I ought to find out why Jeff thinks I can help you. I've got no time to talk football."

"Nothing to do with football. I left the Hawks a while ago and now I'm at OPUS, the new commission on Puget Sound—you could have heard about it?"

"Maybe. Commissions got fancy names, but that's about it. Why'd Jeff think you'd get anything useful from a cop on the other side of the mountains?"

"Okay. Logging's always a hot-button issue. There's a site at Isadka Valley that's got special issues that could affect all logging sites state-wide. I know it's not in your jurisdiction, but its ownership is what Jeff thought might interest you."

"I'm listening."

Gary explained small parcel exemptions and the possible connection between Isadka Valley and the Gideon slide.

"So, Curt Longcart controlled some parcels at Gideon. The same thing could be happening at Isadka, only this time there might be another layer behind Curt. Possibly Grant Tomson. That's why Jeff said I ought to talk to you."

McHugh sounded like he had to work to keep his voice level.

"Damn right. That's one guilty bastard who shouldn't get away with anything more."

"Jeff told me a little about what happened over there."

"Yeah, Tomson walked away from assault and possible complicity in his brother's death. I'd be happy to nail him on anything. You got something serious on him?"

"Nothing solid yet, maybe soon. I hear Tomson's a real piece of work, and if I dig further, he might retaliate. But cops in other jurisdictions don't have your history with Tomson, and might not take a request from me seriously in case I need help."

"I hear you. Make the local call first if there's trouble. Then call me, and I'll call the local jurisdiction, see what I can do to convince them, if that's required."

"Thanks. That's all I wanted."

He was about to end the conversation when McHugh spoke again.

"I get the need for ecological concerns. You know—old growth, second growth, good forestry practices. There's upsides and downsides. The downside's usually the type of people who take over. Some people are like cancer. Tomson's one of those. Actually thought we had a chance to cut him out, you know, convict him. Didn't happen. Now you tell me the rotten shit could be coming back. Be a pleasure if we could really get rid of him this time."

Gary was quiet, absorbing the unexpected response. McHugh went on.

"I know you're Salish. Some of the sports stories mentioned that."

Gary was glad he hadn't used his heritage as a calling card. Now they could both relax.

"Yeah, reporters like colorful identities. Makes their job easier."

"I've gotten some of that 'local Indian' stuff myself. That your uncle Fred, used to live in Bellingham, now's in Yakima?"

"Fred. Yeah. Quite the mouth on him. He's actually less Indian than I am, but you'd never know that to hear him."

They both laughed. McHugh came back, serious again.

"I want Tomson, so don't hesitate to call when you think you've got something important on him. I've got your back if you need me."

Gary punched off and took a final look at the screen. It felt good to know he could count on that number.

NOVEMBER 24

Laura ran through her options—manufactured excuses, really—for contacting Curt Longcart again. Any personal excuse she could think of would sound phony, either putting him on guard or making him ignore her altogether.

The best approach would also be the least complicated: present herself truthfully as an employee of Natural Resources. If Longcart turned her down, she'd report that to her boss, and someone else could follow up. If he did talk to her and reveal anything new, she could report that too. Either way, she would have gone as far as she could on her own.

She punched in the number for Longcart Motors. A receptionist answered, and she asked to speak to Mr. Longcart. A different female voice came on, folksy and friendly.

"Sorry to say that that Mr. Longcart is out of town and won't be back for a few days."

"Is he reachable now?"

"Not unless it's an emergency. He's in Spokane, working on a new advertising campaign."

"Can't say it's urgent right now, but it could be soon. Real soon. He's not going to want to miss this, so if I do have to reach him in a hurry, what's a number I can use?"

She could almost hear the calculation. Laura bet that she wasn't the first person calling anonymously, wanting to contact Longcart. This lady could get into trouble if she stopped an important call.

The folksiness was gone and a guarded voice took over.

"All right. If it's an emergency—and only then—you can call Curry and Edson, a PR firm. He still might not be able to talk; it depends. Wait, I'll get you the number."

Laura's felt her juices flowing. A call to Longcart's PR agency might stir the pot. She could keep up the anonymity, see what happened.

Another thought pushed through. She had promised Gary to stay in touch. Okay. But wait and see if she got some reaction from Longcart. Then she'd call him.

159

She phoned Curry and Edson. As expected, the person who answered was courteous but off-putting. Mr. Longcart was not available. Would she like his voice mail? Why not?

She made a decision. No more cat and mouse. Besides, the risk was small. Voice mails take a while to be checked.

"Hello Curt Longcart. This is Laura Dickens, the lady who dropped by your lot about two weeks ago and asked to meet you. You showed me new models. Yes, I was interested in a new car, but also something else. I work with Natural Resources, and I'd like to talk about Isadka Valley."

She left her cell phone number.

✳ ✳ ✳

Two days now, and still no word from Key. Crash had come home from work after the meeting with Suzanne to find her things gone. Nothing else was disturbed, so she probably left on her own. It was already clear that she wanted to. It hurt, though, that she hadn't left a note.

He wanted to fall back on his default action and drop Key into the mental bin labeled "interesting but done with." She'd have a lot of company there—excursions into promising territory that ultimately deflated or petered out. But to put her there, he'd have to decide that things between them were over. He would have to stop caring, and he just couldn't do that. Not without giving it one more try.

She could be anywhere, but back at the old house by AlkiSteel was most likely. A shot in the dark, but what else did he have?

When he reached the place, he was surprised to see its front door open and a rent-a-cop from the steel mill seated on the steps. As Crash approached, the man stood. His stance and the holster on his hip said former military, and he was big.

"You looking for something?"

"I'm looking for Key. Is she inside?"

"That depends."

Crash was tired of sparring with everything. He took a step forward and looked firmly at the guard.

160

"Tell her that Crash needs to talk to her urgently."

The man sized him up, turned away, and disappeared into the house. Nothing happened for several minutes. Finally, the guard returned, walked away from the house, and stopped. He was out of hearing range but made a point of keeping his hand near his holster.

Crash saw Key just inside the doorway. Her crossed arms and unyielding expression spoke volumes. He climbed the half dozen front steps, stopping on the highest one, just short of the porch.

Key broke the silence, her head lowered. He could barely see her eyes through the curtain of bangs over them.

"What do you want?"

"First, to see you're okay."

"See for yourself."

She was trying to sound dismissive.

"I thought we were working on something important."

"Still am. No 'we' anymore."

"Can you tell me why?"

"You got your life and I got mine."

She finally raised her head.

"Look, I appreciate how you helped me out, but it's time to get things back to where they were. That's my choice."

Tough was losing some of its edge.

"But bad people may still be after you."

She pointed toward the guard.

"Taken care of. A new security system is in the works."

He'd faced moments like this before. If you drift into things, sometimes they work, but most of the time they don't. He'd been told off lots of times. Usually it was easy to move on to something else. This time, he acted.

Before Key had a chance to object, he mounted the stairs and took two long strides to stand right on the door sill. He wasn't in the house, but she couldn't close the door.

Behind them, the guard yelled. Key waved him off.

"What do you want?"

"I just want to say a couple of things. Then I'll leave."

161

"Then say them and go."

He took a deep breath.

"If you really don't want me around, that's your decision; but you've still got the tape, and those crooks will not stop trying to get it. The only way to be safe is to find out who they are and get the police to act. But they can't act without the information we're trying to get. Why stop now? You may not want me close, and that's fine, but we need to stay in touch. All I ask is you take my calls and let me know what you find out. And I'm here for whatever help you need. Agreed?"

When he stopped, he felt as if he'd just heard another person talking. That couldn't be him, could it? Throwing out so much all at once and putting so much passion behind it? He'd just guaranteed rejection.

"Okay."

His heart rose too quickly, and she immediately dashed his hopes for more.

"But I don't want you to come back here uninvited. I've got my life to live, and you've got yours."

Crash felt the return of a dull ache starting somewhere around his breastbone, but tried his best not to let it show.

Neither of them had moved. Key looked away, then back.

"You heard of Gary Seasons, the football player?"

The question startled him. What could it have to do with anything?

"As a matter of fact, yeah. Know him sorta. Installed a sound system in his house. Why?"

Key lowered her voice.

"Suzanne and I talked. She told me one thing that might help. She said that Seasons used to work for Curt Longcart and knows a lot about his business. And he and Longcart might not be on good terms anymore. She suggested getting his help. But..."

"Go on."

"I'm suspicious. You know that. My dad mentioned Longcart a couple of times. He put money into logging. I wonder if he's the one who sent people here to find the tape. Maybe you want to, you know, check into that."

162

Used cars, logging, the tape. Two big jumps with a lot of empty space in between. But his heart was in charge again. Anything to keep him in contact with Key.

"I will."

She paused and looked away and back before she nodded.

"Okay."

"If I can find a way to talk to Gary Seasons, you want to be there?"

"Depends, but maybe, yeah."

That would have to do for now. On his way back to the parking lot, Crash passed the guard, who tracked him briefly and then returned his gaze to the house.

NOVEMBER 27

Mid-morning, and Key hesitated at the bedroom doorway. She still wasn't sure it had been the right move to invite Flora to join her in Seattle. She only knew it seemed right at the time.

A few days ago, she had thought again about how she'd left Flora after the attack at the powwow. Key felt the need to do something. Maybe Seattle would give Flora a temporary break from her situation.

When she called her friend and made the invitation, despair had nearly cancelled Flora's voice, confirming Key's own doubts.

"Nothing'll change. My life's shit here and it'll be shit there."

"You won't know that until you try."

The reply was so weak Key had had to strain to hear it.

"Time comes…too much…try again."

Flora's voice carried the damage that comes from growing up in the middle of hopelessness, punctuated by alcohol and violence. Silence buzzed faintly in the ozone, as if words could no longer bear the weight of defeat. When they continued, they were barely a whisper.

"Besides, I got no money."

Key tried again, replacing doubt with a strengthened urge to do what was right.

"I didn't say you had to move here, you know. Just a few days to rest up. I'll pay for the bus ticket from this end. Won't cost you."

No response.

"C'mon, Flora, why not? Besides, I've been thinking, and maybe I see things differently, especially after what happened at the powwow. All that's been happening for a long time. When you get here, I want to talk. We can't do that up there where you are. Please say yes."

The phone was silent. Key wondered if the connection had been lost. The next sound was a long exhale.

"Tell me how."

Eight hours later, a Bolt Bus had pulled up in front of Union Station on a moonless night, with a cold wind blowing over the top of Century Field. The station itself had closed an hour ago, and only widely-spaced low-voltage lights illuminated the sidewalk that ran along its front. Flora was the last person to get off, carrying a small duffel bag; she shook her head when Key asked if she had any more

167

luggage. They didn't hug each other. That had never been part of their style. But looking at Flora, the remnant of a large bruise still there on her cheek, Key had touched her arm. Back at the big house, Flora had gone right to bed.

Pulling her thoughts back to the present, she heard a sound from the bedroom and cracked the door open quietly to peek in.

An irritated voice called out.

"Whaddya want?"

"Hi Flora. Wanted to see if you're okay."

A snort.

"Now you ask."

"That's not true. We talked a lot by the campfire."

"Talk's cheap. You go up there, get me in bad trouble, and take off."

"I got banged up, too. Just getting back to normal."

"Yeah. Sorry for the interruption of your great life. At least you don't have brothers who rough you up just for making their friends mad. I never should have met you at the powwow. You're not one of us. Never have been."

Key held up a palm to show she got it, turned and left to return to the basement.

She was sitting at her computer a half hour later when Flora came down the stairs. Key offered breakfast. When Flora finished eating, she rose and wordlessly walked around the open basement space, looking at the work table and the objects on it, at the sleeping room and kitchen area.

She opened cabinet and closet doors, looking at the contents, as if she were mentally cataloguing it all.

Key stood off to the side, waiting, increasingly nervous about how to act when Flora's tour was done. But her friend simply walked over to the couch, lay down on her back, and pulled a pillow under her head.

She didn't seem to be asleep. Key took a seat at her worktable and began surfing the net, looking through her blogs one by one for new comments. Her concentration wavered, and she looked over her shoulder to see Flora standing behind her.

"This how you spend your free time?"

"Some of it."

Flora leaned closer. The creases on her forehead and around her mouth were still noticeable, though a good night's sleep had softened them.

"Tell me about it."

Key was astounded to hear undisguised curiosity. She motioned for Flora to grab a chair. Flora sat down and leaned in. Key took her on a tour of her various blogs, explaining how she used different aliases. She glanced from time to time at her friend, whose eyes were following closely.

Finally, Flora sat back.

"No one reads blogs any more. You'd be better off with Medium, or Twitter if you don't need much space. That's something I know about."

Then she got up and went back to the couch again.

At the table, Key relaxed a bit. Sharing her hobby with a friend felt right, even touching. That feeling meant more than any pleasure she got from blogging alone. Flora's reaction shone a new light on things.

What harm was there in continuing, maybe even in trying those other things—Medium, Twitter, whatever?

Why not? If they built a bridge to Flora, it would be worth it.

NOVEMBER 28

Gary slumped in one of the missionary chairs in his living room. A day in the office could tire him more than double football practices or tramping around a forest site.

There had to be a better way. OPUS was a great idea—getting businesses, government, and tribes to work together to protect Puget Sound. But it would accomplish nothing if it just amounted to more talk. Like today.

He'd spent hours talking to commission members about Isadka Valley. They were almost evenly split between those who wanted to go ahead with the current proposal, and those who thought that small parcel exemptions should not be allowed as part of a larger proposal. Predictably, the business-oriented members wanted to allow the exemptions, while government agencies and environmental groups urged caution.

The resulting impasse was beginning to feel unmovable. Unless new evidence was found, this issue would be sidestepped in a final report. By default, it would fade, then become a small problem in the usual tug-of-war between development and regulation. In that end contest, development almost always won.

Forget it. Just thinking about it tired him more. He'd hoped maybe to take Laura to dinner. But he'd called twice and, so far, no response. He tried to lose himself in a new release on Netflix.

Around 9 pm his phone buzzed. He thought it might be Laura but didn't recognize the number. More by reflex than by choice, he punched on.

"Gary Seasons?"

Could be just a solicitation. He almost hung up.

"Yeah. Who's this?"

"My name's Crash Davies."

"Who?"

The voice rushed on, words stumbling over each other.

"I put in your audio system. I play in a band, too, which you said you wanted to hear sometime. Maybe you remember. We're playing tonight."

Gary glanced at the stacked audio components in the open-door cabinet under his TV. A dim recollection followed. Small guy, smart, a little too talkative, but competent.

He started to decline, but this Crash person went on.

"Actually, there's more. I've heard talk about connections between Longcart Motors and Isadka Valley, and your name was mentioned. Just thought you might want to know."

Gary hesitated. Instinct warned that this could be a ploy to compromise him. Yet something in the tone of voice grabbed him.

"Why would I be interested?"

"I saw on the web that you're working for OPUS. And what happened at Gideon might be important to OPUS."

Gary felt a jolt.

"Could be. But I'd need to hear more before deciding that."

"I understand. Are you a night owl?"

Weird question. But what was the harm?

"Generally."

"I'm playing in a bar in West Seattle. We finish at eleven. After that we could meet. Get here before eleven, and you could catch the last set. I'm the guy on bass."

At twenty to eleven, Gary walked into The Crow's Nest on California Avenue, across from the Admiral Theater. The crowd was thinning in the railroad-car-shaped restaurant, booths along one side, a bar and an enclosed kitchen on the other. In a corner by the front door, the trio barely fit on a tiny triangular stage. The drummer had to make do with a snare and a small kick drum.

From a seat at the bar, Gary focused on the electric bass player. Like the music, he was competent but not flashy. His small frame and sandy-orange hair matched a dim memory of the man who'd installed his audio system. Dressed in jeans, a T-shirt, and a red waiter's jacket, sleeves rolled halfway up, nothing else about him seemed memorable or even noticeable.

Gary let his eyes roam the room. At the end of the bar, they stopped moving. In the last seat by the opening to the kitchen, a young woman sent off signals that she wanted to be left alone. He caught a brief glimpse of her face and wondered if she might be part Indian. Another woman, tiny, appeared from the rear of the room and approached the one at the bar. They talked for a few moments, their heads almost touching. Then the tiny woman retraced her steps and disappeared.

When the band stopped, all but a few customers paid up and left. Gary moved to a vacated booth near the rear. He sat down and almost immediately the bass player joined him.

"Hello, Gary."

"I remember you now. Crash."

Gary searched the blue eyes for any hint of deception, but saw none. He waited until Crash spoke again.

"I have some things to tell you. About Isadka Valley, like I promised. The woman at the bar, and another one in the kitchen, can speak firsthand about what's going on there. Can you wait until they join us? Shouldn't be long."

"Do I have a choice?'

"Sure. But I think you're gonna want to hear what they say."

Gary nursed his beer uneasily. More people involved could also mean complications. Crash stayed silent until the women came over and sat. Then he started right in.

"Key and Flora, this is Gary. Gary, these are the people who know about what happened at Gideon."

The main vibe both women gave off was reluctance, if not downright suspicion. Crash went on with a summary: a break-in at Key's house and an unprovoked attack at a powwow. He explained that Curt Longcart might be one of the voices in a taped conversation that could be incriminating. Gary perked up at that.

"Where's the tape now?"

Key spoke up.

"As if I'll tell you."

"I'm not asking for it. But you must have heard it. Is it genuine?"

"You doubting me? My father gave it to me. He died because of Gideon."

Gary decided to try another tack.

175

"Flora, would I know any of the people who beat you up?"

His heritage had not been mentioned, but he was pretty sure Flora had figured that out.

She raised her eyes to his, and he saw the damage there. That look could be found anywhere, but he'd seen it more in the eyes of kids and women than in men. The men's eyes more often lit up with hatred.

"I knew most of them."

"Indians?"

"Some, not all."

"Anyone in particular?"

Now they were speaking as if Key and Crash weren't with them.

"Clif Lerman. He didn't beat me up, but he spoke to the powwow. I can't prove it, but I bet he told the others what to do."

"Wouldn't be surprised. Clif, yeah I know him, used to hang around Longcart Motors. Know his half-brother, too, Derek Bowman. That's a seriously bad dude."

He meant those words only for Flora, but glanced at Key as he spoke and thought he saw her expression change.

"Anything else?"

Crash jumped in.

"There's a possibility that Grant Tomson's involved with Isadka Valley too. And we've discovered…"

Gary saw him flick a glance at Key.

"…that the Triplets—you know the bunch that does Longcart commercials? —maybe have been helping him keep the Isadka Valley project on track. Blogging in his favor. Maybe trying to find out where Key is. We don't know for sure, but the Triplets' leader is willing to switch sides."

"Switch sides? What does that mean, and why would they do that?"

Crash shook his head.

"Switching sides means writing about different topics. You know, environmental safety, Indian rights. Why? Maybe they're worried about their careers."

"Maybe. That's weak. These are high-stakes issues. You got to be more sure than that about people's motives. Are you sure about theirs?"

"I hear you. Like I said, no harm so far. We'll be careful."

After a pause, Crash got going again.

"But if we use the Triplets right, maybe we can get Longcart to show more of what he's up to. Could help us find out about Isadka and about what happened earlier at Gideon. That's what Key's most interested in. Her dad died because he knew too much about Gideon."

Gary saw Crash flash a look in Key's direction and couldn't miss her scowl in return. Too much information, a lot of it vague. He tried to slow things down.

"Look, these are powerful people with powerful money. And you think blogging to a small audience is going to stop them? What else you got?"

Flora spoke up.

"I might get us a bigger audience."

The comment surprised Gary and, by the look on his face, surprised Crash, too. Key smiled.

"I didn't even know you had a computer."

Flora went on.

"I talk to people online. Been at it for a while now. I've got a pretty big following on Twitter. Enough to increase your blog traffic."

Gary shook his head.

"But what's the end game? Stop the Isadka project? Expose some mysterious information that proves it's another Gideon? If you have the tape with Longcart's voice on it, why not take it to the police? Or the media? They could force his hand better than any blog ever could."

No one responded. The conversation was losing its energy. Gary sighed.

"You've given me pieces of information, but they're vague and disconnected. I appreciate it, but there's nothing definite enough for me or OPUS to act on. Yet. Glad to have met you, and I hope you'll let me know if something important comes up."

They said a few things about staying in touch, and then left.

Alone, Gary asked himself whether this chunk out of his sleep time had been worth anything. These amateurs were working against professionals. They wanted to do something positive about Isadka Valley. But were they aware enough to protect themselves?

NOVEMBER 29

Toward the end of morning shift, Crash heaved the heavy mop head rhythmically across the smooth concrete floors of the glass studio. As he worked, he let his mind catalogue the matters that he, or at least someone, ought to keep track of. Gary at OPUS; Suzanne and the Triplets; and of course Key, if she would let him.

He was thinking of taking a break when his cell phone rang. He recognized the number and almost decided to let the call go to voice mail. He wasn't in the mood for Suzanne. On the fifth buzz, he relented.

"This is Crash."

He would have recognized her flighty sound even without the first words.

"It's Suzanne. I need to talk to Key. I've got some ideas about the blog thing, but I have no way of reaching her except through her blog, and she's not responding. Want to be the carrier pigeon?"

"What should I tell her?"

"Just that I'm trying to hold up my end of the bargain. Give her my number. She can call me. If she doesn't, I'll assume this whole thing is dead. Which is fine. I don't have time for any coy act."

Petulance rippled through the words. She recited her cell number and thanked him before hanging up.

He took a bathroom break, grabbed a candy bar from the machine, and finished mopping the area in front of the furnace while he thought.

He'd been encouraged when Key was willing to meet with Gary Seasons. He'd hoped it would lead to more encounters with her. Hadn't turned out that way, though.

He could drive over to the house and deliver Suzanne's message in person, but Key had told him not to go back there. If he showed up she'd push him away for sure. Might not answer the phone, either. But he should try. Before he could change his mind, he grabbed his phone and walked outside.

To his surprise, she answered on the third ring.

"What is it?"

Annoyance.

"Hey, Key. Suzanne called. She needs to get hold of you. I wanted to come over to tell you, but…"

He let the words hang. She ignored the opening.

"I saw her comments on the blog. Just didn't want to answer at the moment."

"That's fine, but she seems to really want to talk to you now. I'll text you her number."

Key grunted a reply. Then, she cleared her throat.

"Thanks."

Was that the first time she'd ever thanked him? It was, at least, a small glimpse of encouragement. He settled on a simple goodbye and sent her Suzanne's number. Then he returned to his mop.

❀ ❀ ❀

Key tried to control herself as she spoke into her cell.

"No, Suzanne, I don't think that's a good idea. Seattle maybe. But North Creek? We could meet when you get back."

"Oh come on, Key. It's only half an hour. The weather's supposed to be nice."

Could be okay. Rain wasn't due to return until late tomorrow. She still fought the idea of putting Suzanne in charge. Partly she was reacting to the tone of an email from Suzanne she had received through her blog.

The email spelled out how to use Twitter to raise awareness of Isadka Valley and its potential to become another Gideon. Key saw what Suzanne was getting at—trying to make a message go viral. Get all the dirt they currently had and blast it on Twitter, Facebook, Instagram—every conceivable site. Flora had a lot of followers, which could be the start. Then they'd have to hope the message gained traction so that responses built across social media. Next, alternative news sites might pick it up and run with it, starting their own investigations and hopefully leading to coverage by major media outlets.

But this plan assumed a lot. Going viral on purpose was almost impossible. Most likely they'd get a few shares and a sympathetic blurb on a site no one read. Then it would die out. Meanwhile, some nonsense item like a sneezing panda would end up on the news, and Isadka Valley would be logged, lives would be in danger, and the bad guys would win.

As she read, Key thought, too, about her father's tape. Up to now it had been like a dangerous souvenir. She wanted to keep it as a connection to him. Now she realized that, along with the media exposure about Isadka, the tape could be put to positive use. But that was for later.

In the meantime, doing something was better than doing nothing. Key had to admit that Suzanne's plan was enticing. She might even be sincere.

Suzanne kept talking on the phone. Impatience was taking control of her voice.

"I thought you and your friends needed to get something started right away, so I'm the one making time for you. My bad, that I didn't rearrange my whole schedule for you. But I've got time pressures, too. The troupe I'm in is setting up a new theater in a converted barn in North Creek, and I have to be there today and tomorrow. But I can make time to meet, and I know a place that serves a good brunch. Can we meet tomorrow up there?"

Key bristled but waited for her own irritation to subside. Their whole idea about building an audience could bomb, but they wouldn't know unless they stuck with it a while longer. So the meeting—not the time, place, or convenience—took priority. And she thought Flora would like the idea, which was added incentive.

"Okay. Just give me the address, and I'll be there."

"I'll text it later."

"And I might bring a friend."

Key heard a throaty laugh.

"Deal."

Key climbed from the basement to the first floor and knocked on Flora's closed door. A timid voice reached her with the message to come in.

She and Flora were getting along better, finding an adult connection that transcended what they'd known about each other as kids. To her surprise, on the third morning of Flora's visit Key woke up with a sense of pleasure that her friend was there. Someone else was close; and, instead of that presence feeling intrusive or threatening, it was beginning to feel natural.

Flora sat in a straight-back chair by the window, a roller blind up just a few inches to allow some light in. An open book lay across her knees.

"Good morning. Sleep well?"

"Better."

Not needing to use a lot of words was another thing that felt easy for both of them. Key sat on the bed and waited. Silence didn't mean that communication had stopped. A shy smile said a lot, and the relaxed look around Flora's eyes said even more. Words started, two or three, gradually a conversation. Key told her about the phone call. Flora listened and, halfway through the account, closed her book.

"It's a long shot, but what do we have to lose? I'll come with you to meet Suzanne. She's in entertainment. We can combine our followers online and speed up spreading the word."

Key was encouraged.

"You really want to come?"

Flora smiled.

"A drive'd be nice. Like old times—you and me cruising around after school."

She left Flora and returned to the basement. Another thought licked at her. She had promised Crash that they'd keep in touch about Suzanne. She owed him a text message.

But she wouldn't invite him along.

❋ ❋ ❋

Laura was surprised by the morning call. Curt Longcart went straight to the point.

"I guessed you were after something else when you came to the showroom."

"You were right. I'm working on logging site assessments and thought it would be easiest to talk to you informally. My visit to your showroom was a clumsy first step. Can we start over?"

He paused, but not for long.

"Tell you what, Ms. Dickens: I don't want to make you come all the way up here again. Let's talk where we can relax. You know the Paradise on Magnolia? They serve good food. Why not let me take you to dinner? How about tonight? Short notice, I know, but this is a busy time of year for me, and it might be a while before we get another chance. Have to be a little late—maybe around nine?"

Alarm bells sounded, but not all that loud. Longcart was going out of his way to be accommodating. She didn't take long to decide.

"That'll work."

"Just one thing. What I'm going to tell you, I might not want to share with anyone I don't know. So let's make dinner for just the two of us. Okay?"

"Agreed. But I'll pay for my meal."

At 9 pm, Laura surveyed the Paradise Café. It was a popular place, otherwise she would have backed off from Curt's invitation. There was an empty seat opposite her at a table for two.

The restaurant was one of those places where some diners dressed up and others wore whatever they'd had on all day. She'd stayed in jeans and added a nice blouse. A rain parka was the only sensible choice for a night like this, with drizzle already falling and heavier rain expected later.

Her earlier faint suspicion had urged her to do one thing more before she left her apartment. She had searched a drawer and found a small metal cylinder, a voice-activated recorder with a built-in mic that she'd used for college lectures. She tucked it into the mesh pocket of her parka. She might want to use it, or not. But at least she'd have it. She made sure of fresh batteries.

She'd also tried Gary's cell number and got sent to voice mail. Her message was brief.

"Gary, it's Laura. I have a meeting with Curt Longcart tonight. No idea how that's going to go, but…"

185

She hesitated before adding a final sentence.

"I'm eager to tell you how it works out."

Her eyes were on the front door of the Paradise when it opened and Longcart strode in. He saw her, walked over, sat, and smiled, all affability.

"I was kind of out of sorts the other day and showed it. That's not like me, and I don't like the impression it made."

Might as well cut to the chase.

"Didn't notice. Would you be willing to talk about Isadka Valley?"

❉ ❉ ❉

"I'm eager to tell you how it works out."

That was the end of Laura's voice mail. Damn. Why had he forgotten his phone in the car last night? The time stamp was 8:06 pm, just after he'd come back from the market and turned on the TV to watch a movie.

Gary listened to the whole message again. The final sentence gave him a lift, but then worry set in that she'd gone too far by contacting Curt.

He wasn't sure what to do. Normally, Sunday was for house chores. Nothing here was urgent enough to demand attention, though.

It didn't take long to decide. Laura had described where she lived in enough detail that he was pretty sure he could find her building. If he hadn't heard from her by tomorrow morning, he'd go there first thing.

Meanwhile, a nagging question elbowed in. Had he been definite enough in warning her about Longcart?

NOVEMBER 30

Rory Edwards. Crash's memory coughed up the name. According to Suzanne, Edwards had put the Triplets up to harassing Key on the web. But why would a PR guy in Spokane care about logging or Indians? Crash needed to find out more.

With Key looking out for herself, Sunday was like a hole in his life. He left Seattle early, heading east on I-90 toward Spokane.

Local traffic had mostly pulled off at the second Esterville exit, and only widely-spaced vehicles traveled a flat, open expanse. With a local country western station as his companion and the morning sun peeking through occasional breaks in a leaden sky, he crossed the Columbia River.

Before leaving, he'd seen a text from Key. It simply said she'd be meeting Suzanne in North Creek, the exit he'd passed more than an hour ago. No invitation for him to join. He had to make a real effort to push away that lingering feeling of disappointment.

It hadn't been hard to find Edwards' address in a small town called Manoway, near Spokane. The drive was long but smooth, and he was surprised when a sign informed him that he had to exit the interstate in ten miles. If he missed that exit, he would hit the outskirts of Spokane in fifteen minutes.

Off the interstate, he drove on a two-lane that went straight north about ten miles. Manoway, when he reached it, turned out to be a huddled collection of small subdivision houses. He had no clue what could be supporting the residents. There might be some ranches scattered on the low hills behind the settlement. On one hill, he saw rows of wine grapes. Wineries were a growth industry in Washington, though he doubted the harvest from this place would win any medals. Most likely, the majority of Manoway's inhabitants worked in Spokane.

The house Crash sought was at the end of a short street with only a few other houses on it. There was no turn-around of the type you saw in subdivisions. The pavement just stopped, and the scrub-covered expanse beyond it took over. Edwards' front yard was browned-out grass and nothing else. The house hunkered down, silent, curtains drawn. A slatted six-foot fence surrounded a back yard about as large as the house itself.

189

Reality sank in: Crash was about to meet a man he knew nothing about. He could be an axe-wielding psychopath—although it was doubtful; all other accountants he'd met were far from that.

Curiosity won out; he parked halfway up the block and approached the house. No one answered his knock, so he walked around one side to the fenced yard and found a hinged gate cracked open.

What he saw was like a surreal and precise Magrit painting. The back yard was a perfect square of brown grass and grey weathered fence. In its exact center, a man sat on a bench upholstered in shiny yellow vinyl, holding a cup and facing a bright winter sun. From this angle he could see no face, only the shoulders of a red parka and a head of silver hair. Nothing moved. The scene stayed motionless for a full minute.

In the few times he had gotten close to a dangerous situation, Crash always made sure he had a back door. Today's back door, his car, was a block away. His shallow breathing sounded like the start of hurricane season, and his heart pounded with the force of big waves to follow. Slowly he opened the gate, and his feet moved him into the yard. He spoke softly, hardly hearing the sound of his own voice.

"Rory Edwards?"

The man dropped his cup, leapt forward, crouched and turned all in one movement. He hunkered so low that Crash could see only his shoulders and head. His eyes expanded with terror.

Crash raised his voice, keeping it calm.

"I just wanted to talk to you. About the Triplets."

With that, the man shot up and, half stumbling, ran the twenty feet to the rear fence. He put his hands up to avoid crashing, righted and turned. His arms found a horizontal stringer that held him up. It was weird, but the image of a crucifix came and went.

Now Crash could assess him. Thin, with clothes that seemed too big. Sparse, light hair lying listlessly over a pinched, elongated face. If the arms were anything like the hands he saw, they would be thin and flaccid, hardly weapons to be feared.

He was about to say something when a wail emerged from the man's lips.

"I knew this would happen. I didn't want to do it. I just wanted to be left alone. They wouldn't leave me alone. It wasn't my fault."

Crash kept his distance, trying to make sense of what he was hearing.

"Who are 'they'?"

The man's breathing calmed down a bit.

"Suzanne sometimes talked about a guy named Clif. Otherwise, I didn't ask. What's the difference?"

"But you did pass instructions on to the Triplets?"

Edwards dropped his arms, and a look of genuine surprise appeared.

"What?"

"Suzanne said you were the one who told them what to write. You were controlling them."

Edwards turned angry.

"The bitch. She said that?"

Now Crash felt confused.

Edwards took a step away from the fence.

"I'm just an accountant. I did some stupid things in Montana, and people used that to make me do other things for them."

"What things?"

"Small stuff. Adding signatures to documents they should've signed, or back-dating payments."

"Who?"

"Mostly Curt Longcart. That stopped when I moved to Spokane."

"And Longcart had you pass on instructions to the Triplets?"

Edwards looked puzzled, then allowed a small smile.

"I get it. You think Suzanne was leaned on."

Edwards laughed. A thin, taunting laugh.

Crash felt a constriction moving up his spine toward the base of his neck.

"If she wasn't, then…"

Edwards' smile changed to a sneer.

"Welcome to the club."

"She was in charge?"

191

A glint of defiance flared in Edwards' washed-out eyes. He stood straight now, his hands swallowed by baggy sleeves.

"Surprised? That was me, too, after I first met her. She has that flighty act down perfect. Underneath there's a mean cougar with claws. She runs the other two, her cousins, like they was puppets. Hell, she ran me. My only job was to give her cover, to take the fall if things went sour."

"But you're not doing that now."

"Way I figure, it's too late. It's over. I'll get what I got coming."

"Can't see how you've done anything wrong."

"That's not what some people will think. I've said enough. Too much, probably. Leave me alone."

Crash hardly heard the last words. His mind was already far away. If Suzanne was behind the Triplets and their blogs, then she'd been playing them the whole time. But Key didn't know that...

He didn't want to finish the thought.

He punched up Key's cell, but it went immediately to voice mail. Now he was running toward the gate. Behind him Edwards was laughing.

❀ ❀ ❀

This had to be the building, Gary thought. About where Laura described it. And it was one of those new micro-apartment buildings, like she said.

He parked and went to the entrance. Laura's name was easy to find on the occupants' list. He rang and waited. No response.

Despite a growing impatience, he'd purposely waited until afternoon before going to the apartment, hoping she'd call first. He'd made a private bet that she would. When she didn't, instinct kicked in and now a small worry had grown into something larger.

At that moment his phone rang, and he answered quickly.

The words were so rushed that he had trouble understanding them. He'd almost hung up when he heard the name "Longcart".

"Slow down. Who is this?"

"It's Crash Davies. You know, the guy who put in your audio system? I'm on I-90 east of the pass. You're the only person I've been able to reach."

"Yeah, Crash. I can barely hear you. Pull over so you can tell me what's up."

The engine sound decreased, and he could hear better.

"Remember we talked about the Triplets, and how they were coerced into harassing Key and blogging favorable stuff about Isadka Valley? And how Suzanne agreed to switch sides? Said she'd only been following orders?"

"Yeah, I remember."

"I just found out she was the one giving the orders. That changes everything. This morning, Key went to North Creek to meet Suzanne, and Flora could be with her. They might be in danger. I'm trying to get there as fast as I can."

His voice was getting hoarse.

Gary kept his voice calm.

"What can I do?"

"I don't know who else to call. If I call the police, my story's too vague."

Gary lowered the phone while he mentally sifted through possibilities.

"Might be someone I could call. How soon before you get to North Creek?"

"About an hour."

"Keep going. I'll try to reach a cop in Swiftwater named McHugh. North Creek's not his jurisdiction, but he may be able to contact local authorities in case you need them. Find out what you can at North Creek and give me a call."

Crash came on one more time.

"Almost forgot. This strange dude I just met mentioned Suzanne worked with a guy named Clif. Maybe the same guy who beat up Key at the powwow?"

Clif again, no more chance of coincidence. Still no word from Laura. Nothing had changed, except that Gary was now on alert for two calls, instead of one.

He'd phone Bill McHugh, the cop in Swiftwater. Then back to waiting.

✳ ✳ ✳

Laura surveyed the white cube of a room, furnished only with a mLaura surveyed the white cube of a room, furnished only with a metal table and a few chairs. Events of the previous evening came back: dinner with Longcart, then being grabbed from behind. Her head ached and she had a sharp, acrid taste in her mouth. Had she been knocked out with chloroform or something?

She heard a lock click, and the door opened. She jumped up, backed into a corner, arms extended.

Longcart entered with a fast-food cardboard tray. She could smell the coffee.

"My, my. Still ready for a fight? Thought that would have gone out of you by now. Thought you might be hungry. People generally say I'm a good host."

He added a smug laugh.

"See, I didn't even tie you up. When I built these offices next to the shop and showroom, I made sure loud noises wouldn't get in. Nothing gets out either."

She made a move to get around the conference table that separated them. Longcart took a quick step backwards, and, without dropping the food, reached back to the door handle with his free hand.

"Uh-uh. No-no. Make another move like that and I'll leave you with no food."

She stopped where she was.

"Good girl. Now you just wait and we'll continue this later."

He left the food on the table, and she heard the click of a lock as the door closed behind him.

Laura looked at the food but made no move toward it. What had happened last night made her feel sick. God, had she been stupid.

Their dinner conversation at the Paradise gave no hint that anything was wrong. She didn't remember the food; she'd come for information. But each time she asked about Isadka Valley, Longcart fended her off or changed the subject. That was irritating, but not surprising. After a while she'd had enough and said she needed to leave. By that time, his friendly-neighbor façade was gone.

"Guess you're getting impatient. I would be too, if I were you."

He leaned forward, his voice dropping into a low, confidential slot.

"I do have information for you. Documents. I couldn't give you them without sizing you up. Wouldn't be the first time that one of my competitors used a pretty girl to get me to lower my guard."

He'd leaned back and smiled.

"You're for real."

The smile gave way to a serious look.

"This isn't easy for me. I've done some things in my business and in my life that I wish I could have back. But none of them includes Isadka. Rumors are making me look bad, and I want to stop them. Can I trust you to read what I give you with an open mind?"

That got her attention. She'd thought of what she might take back with her, how her stock would rise at Natural Resources. Her guard had come down without her even realizing it.

She remembered him paying ostentatiously in cash, leaving a huge tip. His tone was jovial when they walked to the far corner of the parking lot where his car was backed into a spot. She waited by the front of the car while he went to the rear, feeling increasingly confident. The trunk lid rose, and Longcart called out.

"Here they are."

In her excitement, she stepped toward the rear of the car. Out of nowhere, a hand clamped down on her mouth, an arm circled her waist and yanked her off her feet. Surprise cancelled everything except an instinct to stiffen. By the time she started to fight back, she was already a heap in the trunk, and the lid was closing.

Now she sat staring at cooling coffee and a soggy breakfast sandwich that stared back at her in silent rebuke. An inner voice yelled at her for her stupidity. People had told her often enough that she tried to do things by herself too much. Now, for the first time in her life, she realized, she was in a situation where she could not, through her own will and strength, force a way forward—or out.

❋ ❋ ❋

Key woke in complete darkness. She tried to find a comfortable position, but there was no such thing. Whatever she could guess about her surroundings came through smell. Sometime in the past, oils and solvents had been in here. The air around her didn't move at all. Was she in a locker, a place where volatile materials could be stored?

Her hip hurt the most. The floor beneath her was rough concrete with imbedded gravel. Sharp stones poked through and ground into her hip.

The events of the day before replayed in her brain. Suzanne had opened the barn door, chatting excitedly about how perfect it would be for the new theater. Beyond the sliding door it was dark inside. Suzanne motioned for her to go first, and Flora followed. Then the door slid back shut and she heard a muffled cry from Flora. At that exact moment, a bright light shone in her eyes, and a hand grabbed her arm.

In pulling free, she'd broken the bead bracelet on her wrist, then run into the darkness. She plunged from side to side, running blindly. Her feet stumbled on scattered implements, until she ran into something like a sawhorse, and then into a stack of hay bales. The light found her again, tracking her movement, growing brighter. She sensed a presence near her, and smelled a foul mixture of tobacco and alcohol. Then came a sharp pain on the side of her head, and a different kind of darkness arrived.

So here she lay in a puddle of her own pee. The wetness was there when she came back to consciousness, along with a massive headache that still lingered. Flora's body pushed heavily against her. Flora didn't respond to words or to being shoved. Only shallow, rapid breaths confirmed she was alive.

Key tried to ward off thoughts of pain and of disappearing oxygen by stoking her anger toward Suzanne. That didn't work, so she switched to one of her major skills, berating herself. How could she

196

have been so naïve as to blindly trust Suzanne? Normally, suspecting other people's motives was second nature. She missed big, this time.

She shouldn't have brought Flora along. Would this shock be the last straw, make it impossible for her ever to return to a better place? Something else gnawed—a pang that she had no name for. What about Crash? He knew where she'd gone. Not exactly, but close. He had a habit of showing up uninvited, of sticking his dopey neck out where it didn't belong. Would he do it again, or had she pushed him too far away?

She gave the pang a name: regret.

❄ ❄ ❄

Crash couldn't take a chance on the amount of gas remaining in his car, so he pulled off at an exit. As the tank filled, he tried Key once more, only to be sent to voice mail again.

Half an hour later, in light rain, he crossed the pass going west and, twenty minutes after that, swung into North Creek, a valley town strung along one street, with several built-up spurs off it. On larger lots up the slopes he could see clusters of new, larger houses. The place seemed to be doing well. There were no shuttered store fronts.

For him, though, North Creek would always be an old logging town. A new theater, like what Key said Suzanne was helping to build, sounded more like a venture for some city or suburb, but then what did he know? He parked as dusk was arriving and went into a restaurant with folksy touches. Most of the tables were filled. A woman stood behind an old-fashioned cash register; Crash could see she was actually consulting a smartphone tucked into her hand.

He was near panic about Key, and food was not even on his radar. The woman hid impatience, but she heard him out. No, she didn't know anything about a theater being built. Crash pressed further. She scribbled on a note pad, tore off a leaf, and shoved it in his direction.

"Frank Tanaka, Tamarack Real Estate. Does more business around here than anyone else. Should be in his office on Sunday. Biggest day for drop-ins."

Tamarack Real Estate was at the end of the main street, occupying a stand-alone log building with a large sign over the door. A man he presumed to be Tanaka was on the sidewalk, saying goodbye to a couple when Crash approached him. Dusk was changing to darkness.

The wind had risen, driving rain toward where they stood. Tanaka motioned, and Crash followed him into a comfortable waiting area with large photographs of mountain scenery on the walls. When Crash explained what he wanted to talk about, the realtor's welcoming smile faded, but he stayed pleasant.

"Yeah, I know the place. It's an old barn and farmhouse. The owners might have had some plan for it, but then the man died and no one's been around to take care of it. This young woman…What'd you say her name was again?"

"Suzanne Bickers."

"Yeah, sounds right. I've got it written somewhere. Anyway, she came by with ideas about the place, make it into a theater. Full of herself. Talked about celebrity sponsors. Said she was thinking of more theaters. One in Aggregate."

Tanaka paused and a scowl replaced his standard real estate smile.

"Another thing. There was this guy in her car. Badly scarred. Didn't say anything, but I couldn't help looking at him…"

He grimaced at the memory.

"…Anyway, I'm always ready to sell property, but when she mentioned an out-of-the way place like Aggregate, I wrote her off. She had no financing, plus I've got serious doubts if anyone could turn a profit on a theater in this town. Still, you never know. I took her out to have a look at the property. Never saw her again. I'd know about it if the place had been sold. It hasn't."

Crash asked for directions and Tanaka obliged. A short drive led to the address. Nothing much was visible from the road, but a gravel driveway entered a clearing in the woods. In his headlights, the large barn was the first thing he saw, showing its age, hugging the ground. A wooden house beside it seemed in better repair, and he could make out part of a fenced corral behind the buildings.

The house was locked, with roll-down window shades pulled down to the sills. The barn was closed up, too. His flashlight beam found a padlock hanging from a hasp on a large sliding door. Moving closer, he saw that one side of the shackle was cut through. His eyesight blurred and he froze for a second.

When he grabbed the lock, it swiveled without resistance. In a moment he had the sliding door open enough to get in. The space was musty and dark. He slid the door the rest of the way open. With the flashlight, he could see about a third of the space. Nothing there, and no sounds.

Inside, the space felt larger. Small equipment was strewn around a central space, and along the outer walls, his light revealed hay bales and a feed trough. He turned his attention to the left and right of the sliding door. One side was empty; the other held two wood chairs. They were newer than anything else in the place, and the straw around them had been recently trampled.

Beside the chairs, he got down on his hands and knees, his breath like a roar in his ears. He scrabbled in the straw and came up with a short length of nylon cord, both ends neatly cut through. That could mean anything, he told himself, trying not to give in to his worst fears.

Off to the side, he saw a bright blue bead in the scattered straw. Then two yellow ones close together, and near them two reds and a purple—all the colors in the beaded bracelet Key always wore.

Crash sank into the straw, the tiny beads clutched in one fist. He squeezed them as hard as he could, as if they held information that he could force out.

He controlled himself enough to call Gary. By the end he had a lump in his throat.

"Can we call that cop now? We have to do something."

"I will. The scarred man could be Derek Bowman, Clif Lerman's half-brother. He's damaged ex-military. Bad dude."

Crash felt a jolt like a blow to the chest.

"How bad?"

"Rumor is, Bowman's been involved in a string of thefts. He works smart, never been caught for anything major. But he was dumb when

199

he involved Clif. Clif loves to boast. Bowman has secret properties scattered around the Northwest. When he steals something, according to Clif, he'll move it to one of those locations. For sure he has one in the Bitterroots, and another in Aggregate."

"The realtor said Suzanne mentioned Aggregate."

"Could be important. Better call McHugh; but wait, there's something else that figures here."

"Tell me."

"When we were both working for Longcart, I actually went with Clif one weekend to Aggregate. He showed me a cabin that was part of a former logging operation. Said very few people knew about it. Maybe one of Derek's hiding places."

Crash saw where this was going.

"So Key and Flora were invited to North Creek, but the real plan was to take them to Aggregate."

"It's the only possibility I can think of."

"Do you think you could find the cabin Clif showed you?"

"Maybe."

"That sounds like my best bet. I haven't got any others. Tell me what you remember. I'll head there now."

"It's hard to find. How about this: I figure you can't get there in less than two hours. I can be there in under one. You know Aggregate?"

"No."

"Most of it's on one street. City hall's in the middle, in a building that looks like an old car repair shop. Big metal roll-up door on one side. I'll be waiting there at..."

Crash pressed his phone tightly against his ear.

"... let's say 7:30. I'll text you if I find out anything from McHugh."

They broke off the call and Crash consulted the map on his phone. The route that kept him on the interstate was longer, but quicker. Once he was into the rhythm of the road, his mind locked onto Key, where she might be and what could be happening to her. He tried to concentrate on driving, but his imagination knew no bounds.

As if that were not enough pressure, rain arrived. And got worse the farther he drove.

❋ ❋ ❋

Curt Longcart stood in a corner of the small conference room, his arms crossed so tightly across his chest that he could have been hugging himself. Or calming his nerves. A young man stood next to him, his black hair slicked back.

Everyone was looking at the man in front. He bent forward from the waist, arms extended and planted on the conference table. His face was raised toward her, eyes staring. Laura had never met him, but she'd seen pictures. She knew she was looking at Grant Tomson.

He was in his forties, with sharp, aquiline features, dark hair tightly combed to a narrow skull. He was handsome in the same way that a raptor might be called impressive. Dark eyes radiated authority, and everything about his trim figure seemed designed for efficiency. The sheen on his black silk mock-turtleneck shirt glinted back the overhead light as he moved.

When he straightened up, she judged him to be about six feet tall. With his eyes locked on her, he spoke.

"Ah, so this is the girlfriend. What's your name, girlfriend?"

She chose silence.

Tomson matched her stare for a moment, then, hands in the air, he did a pirouette and faced the opposite wall.

"Well, let's see what I do know in case that jogs your memory."

Laura only half heard the words. Her focus was on the voice-activated recorder that she'd slipped into the side mesh pocket of her jacket. When she was alone, she had reached her bound hands as far as she could toward that pocket. By pulling on the jacket, she had gotten one hand on the device and turned it on by feel.

She returned her full attention to Tomson in the middle of a sentence.

"...thought you were so smart. But all you and your friends did was to call attention to yourselves. Someone visited my office and asked for me. An amateur stunt."

Tomson's voice rose and his eyes drilled into hers.

"What do you take me for? Did you think you could mess around in my affairs and I wouldn't notice? Did you think that if I noticed, I'd do nothing?"

A preening ego was on full display.

"So what do you say, Laura Dickens, former rower and employee of Sara Winters?"

Her mind was in gridlock. In his corner, Longcart, looking nervous, attempted an unconvincing grin of triumph. If Curt was unsure of what was in store for him, what hope did she have?

※ ※ ※

Gary pushed the car hard, up I-5 past the municipalities above Seattle and the big sweep around Everett, finally reaching highway 20 heading east toward Aggregate. The road became narrower as it climbed, and the rain drove down harder. His wipers were on high. Through the clear, then blurred, windshield he tried to give his full attention to the slick roadway. Half his brain would not cooperate.

What had been a worry was now a growing certainty that something was terribly wrong with Laura. He didn't know her that well, but one thing was clear: She was straightforward; and if she said she would keep in touch, she meant it. Her silence had turned into a mental warning bell that wouldn't stop ringing.

Another realization drove with him. Laura had become more to him than a colleague. He'd almost decided to act on a growing attraction. But a built-in caution about getting involved with white girls was at work beneath the surface. No surprise. His early training and a succession of put-downs when he got out of line had kept the caution in place. Football groupies didn't count. None of them seemed interested in anything other than casual sex, counting him as a kind of trophy.

He'd allowed himself to think that Laura might be different. Could she get past categories and think of him as a person? Could he, someone who resented being categorized, get beyond categories, too? He was dimly aware of an irony in there, but he had no space for thinking about it.

The warning bell drowned it out, and got louder as he pulled into Aggregate.

❋ ❋ ❋

Through the rain, Crash spotted Aggregate's city hall. Only one building resembled a former body shop. Gary was standing in a recessed entry doing his best to stay dry.

Crash parked and Gary trotted toward him.

Water running down his face, Gary motioned for Crash to roll down the window, and raised his voice to penetrate the curtain of rain.

"Let's take my car. I've got four wheels."

Crash jumped out of his car and into a small SUV. Gary started up and was backing out when he spoke.

"It's not far, but there's a second turn-off after the first one. Hard to spot."

"Get a hold of that cop?"

"Yeah. McHugh said he'd call an officer out here to alert him that we might need help. But it's probably a county officer. Aggregate's too small for its own department. If it's a county matter, it may take a while for someone to get here. I guess we'll find out."

They were less than a mile out of town when Gary swerved into an unmarked gap in the trees and onto a gravel track. Water from large puddles sprayed up onto the windshield and side windows. The next turn was an even smaller opening between two tall firs. Gary missed it on the first pass, backed up, and drove through.

The passage was about a hundred yards long. Halfway up it, Gary switched to parking lights and proceeded at a crawl to the end of the trees where the road widened. He parked off to the side and spoke before opening his door.

"Completely quiet now. Best to assume someone's here even if they're not. This here's a clearing where the building sits."

They moved by foot-feel across an open space, stepping in puddles more than on dry spots. Mud oozed over the tops of Crash's low shoes, and soon he might as well not have had them on. Something loomed in the rain and Gary, in the lead, reached back to stop him, whispering so low that Crash could barely hear.

"Looks like a car. Could just be a junker that's been here a while. The building's not quite like what I remember. Wait here and I'll check it out."

He disappeared and Crash waited. After a minute or two, Gary returned. His face was invisible, but Crash had no trouble hearing him this time.

"No light or sounds. Without a flashlight, I can't tell for sure. But there's nothing to say anyone's been here."

Crash sank to a crouch and felt like sinking all the way into the mud. He didn't want to give up hope—but where was it when he needed it?

Gary crouched beside him.

"I think there were other buildings around here. I'm going back to the car for a flashlight."

Empty space replaced the feel of a body beside Crash. One of his legs was starting to cramp, so he rose and walked a few paces to shake it out. Through the rain, he saw a strobing light; in a few seconds the light steadied and moved closer. Gary's voice came from behind it.

"On the way back from the car, I saw that another road continues up. Hold on to my coat. It's wet and slippery out here."

Gary covered the light with one hand, letting only some of it past his splayed fingers. Crash found the bottom of Gary's coat, gripped it, and matched his stride. They moved slowly up a steeper grade, slipping and righting themselves every few paces. Gary stopped suddenly. Neither one moved. Ahead, a dim oblong of light was barely visible through the rain. Crash's heart rose when he recognized the outline of a window.

Gary had already turned off his flashlight. He started moving forward again, and Crash went with him. When his grip on the coat pulled upwards, he raised his foot and pushed up onto what felt like a concrete slab.

A hazy glow gradually resolved into a rectangle, backlit by dim light. A window must have been cracked open, because they could hear fragments spoken by a raised female voice.

"...you can finish here...I'm needed at...gotta go."

The next moment, Crash heard a door wrenched open. A burst of light from inside was like lightning in the wet darkness. Gary accelerated through the open door, and he followed.

Inside the door was a workroom with several long tables. Three dim bulbs in fixtures hung down from a slanted ceiling. A young woman stood frozen in surprise. Behind her crouched a man with a black pony tail and a horribly scarred face. Crash recognized Suzanne, but only for an instant as she bolted past them out the door.

Scarface charged. He was shorter and leaner than Gary. His right hand flicked a hunting knife back and forth. The speed with which the knife appeared, and the way the man held it, showed he knew how to use it.

The first knife thrust missed as Gary jumped sideways, stumbled and ended up half sprawled over one of the tables. Immediately Scarface came at him again. This time his knife struck Gary's jacket high on his upper right arm. Gary twisted sideways, swinging his left arm in a wide arc. The arm caught Scarface's neck, and Crash heard the wet thump of its impact. The assailant staggered back, his knife dangling at his side. He retreated behind a table as Gary went on the offensive.

Scarface's fierce expression disappeared. Gary was quicker and stronger. The fight went on for another minute, but Crash could tell it was already over.

Scarface could only react. Without warning, Gary leapt onto a table and launched himself feet-first. Scarface tried to back up and was stopped by another table. Too late, he raised his knife. Gary's full weight caught him on the chest, driving him against the table edge. Crash heard a loud crack. It could have been wood or bone. Or both.

Gary kept on moving, lifting and tossing Scarface onto the table-top, where he kneeled on the man's back, grabbed the neck of his shirt, and ripped it off. He tore the shirt into strips and tied Scarface's arms

205

behind his back. That done, he tied the man's ankles. Only then did Gary take off his own jacket and shirt.

Scarface's knife had made a nasty gash in Gary's right bicep, and blood covered his forearm. Following Gary's instructions, Crash tore off more shirt and tied a tourniquet below Gary's shoulder.

Adrenalin fueled Crash's attention during the fight. As soon as it was over, thoughts about Key took over. She wasn't here in this room. But what about the heavy door at the rear? He ran to it and tried the handle. No movement. The door was made of rough, thick planks of hardwood, with oversize hinges made of the same metal as the lock.

He put his ear to the wood and heard nothing. He was about to ask Gary to give a listen, when a different voice, a husky masculine one, surprised him from the doorway.

Rain dripped off the plastic cover over a police officer's hat, and off of the serious D-cell flashlight hanging from one arm. The officer's bearing and voice came straight from a manual.

"My partner and I are here in response to information that we should check out activities at this place."

The policeman's hand moved toward his unbuttoned holster when Gary stood up, revealing the bound man on the table and the blood on his arm. Gary raised his good arm into the air and quickly explained why he and Crash were here and what had happened.

The officer didn't relax, but he did move into the room. At that point, he appeared to recognize Gary.

"You're Gary Seasons? You have reason to believe there are hostages behind that door? McHugh alerted us there might be some."

Crash's heart was pounding so fast that all he could do was nod—and hope.

The policeman followed procedure. He checked on Scarface and made Gary move to a wall so he could be patted down. Only then did his attention shift to the heavy wood door. Crash tried to calm himself.

The officer went outside and returned quickly with a two-foot tool box. He selected a large wrench and went to work on the hinges that were bolted to the door and on the vertical support next to it. The bolts were long; each took an excruciating amount of time to remove.

Crash forced himself to hold still and watch. He tried to concentrate on a second officer who had entered and was leaning over the bound man on the table. Scarface was conscious enough to be talking.

Finally the last bolt fell to the floor with a clatter. The policeman raised a pry bar and worked it into the seam where the door met the lintel. He kept levering the bar until it gave a loud creak and the door fell outward, crashing onto a table, pivoting to the side, and falling hard on the floor. A cloud of dust shot up.

For a moment Crash couldn't see anything, but his feet moved him past the officer and into the open space where the door had been. He stumbled on an object on the floor, and dropped to his knees. Dim light now penetrated the gloom, and he saw two bodies. His heart pounded.

One of the bodies moved. He leaned forward—it was Key! Gently he undid the cloth binding on her wrists and moved his arms underneath her. Her arms rose to circle his neck. Flora lay by her side, curled in a fetal position. Crash struggled up, hanging onto Key, and carried her out into the larger room.

He tried to lower her onto a table, but the grip around his neck grew tighter, and he was conscious of moisture on his chest. So he stood there, holding her, letting her cry.

He could have stood there as long as necessary, holding Key. But gradually another thought picked at his brain: Where was Suzanne?

He looked around and discovered Gary by his side, his sleeve rolled up to reveal flesh-colored tape covering most of his upper arm.

Gary answered the unasked question.

"The police brought along an EMT. These staples'll hold me until I can get stitches."

His expression darkened and he nodded toward Scarface.

"That's Derek Bowman. Claims he doesn't know where Clif is, but I have an idea."

Gary paused long enough to pick up his jacket and check his phone. Scrolling messages, he filled Crash in.

"McHugh, the Swiftwater cop, texted to find out how things are going. He was getting ready to drive to the west side and said he'll head up to Longcart's place, in case he can be of help to local officers. I also got a text from Longcart; he wants to talk."

He looked toward the door.

"There doesn't seem to be anything more we can do here. As soon as the cops are done with me, I'm heading to Lynnwood."

❋ ❋ ❋

Gary didn't bother to knock. The side door at Longcart Motors was unlocked. He'd been through this door countless times. Behind it, he visualized the small waiting area and the conference room beyond that. It was always in the conference room where he and Curt had held what Curt called their "one on one" talks. That was shorthand for being told how things really worked, what he had to do to stay on Curt's good side.

But this confrontation was going to be different.

The waiting room was empty, and the door to the conference room ajar. Apparently McHugh hadn't arrived yet. No reason, though, not to have a talk with Curt.

Gary entered the conference room. Still no Curt. Gary tapped the number on his cell phone. Curt picked up immediately.

"Where are you?"

"In the conference room."

"Be right there."

Less than a minute later, the door opened and Curt came in. On the surface, he was the same old Curt, wearing a cowboy/Indian outfit, pearl button pockets, and a beaded bracelet on his wrist. He didn't shake hands. When he sat down, he looked shrunken and directed his words toward the surface of the table. If he had been a tire, you'd have said he was near flat.

"Got a real problem and I need your help."

That was a first.

"Word's out in the tribes about ownership problems at Isadka. The grumbling's not too loud yet, but I can't let it get worse. Some tribes are thinking about pulling out. They're gettin' nervous that Isadka's being tied to what happened at Gideon."

All of that came out in an unbroken burst. Gary expected to hear more, but Curt veered off in a different direction.

"Ya know, just too much goin' on. We gotta figure out what to do. Don't know about you, but I need a cuppa coffee to help things settle."

Curt reached for his phone.

"Maria, two coffees. Both black. Don't forget the sugar bowl."

He punched off and looked a bit apologetic.

"I know it's not nice to ask staff to stay late, but once I knew you were coming…"

His voice trailed off and silence hung between them for a long minute. The door to the room opened and a dark-haired woman entered, pushing a teacart. There was something familiar about her, but Gary couldn't place her. She had a limp, and looked downward as she served Curt. He tasted the coffee, added sugar, and returned the bowl to the cart. As the woman turned toward Gary, Curt called out in his jovial salesman's voice.

"Hey, Gary. You seen those new models in the showroom? The sports truck in Seahawk blue with sea green accents? Hope to sell a bunch. Give you a great deal if you're interested."

What was that all about? The woman put a cup of coffee at his elbow, and he waved off the offered sugar bowl. Curt's odd behavior grabbed his attention.

He felt a sharp jab in his left triceps, jerked away, and turned. The woman had stepped back. In her raised hand he saw a blurry object that looked like a needle, and under her black hair he thought he saw red strands.

But by then a curtain of unconsciousness was falling all the way down.

✻ ✻ ✻

Crash summoned his strength, but he was losing the fight. He gathered what little resistance he had left and then…woke up. It took a few seconds more to realize that he had not actually been struggling violently with a scar-faced man. Instead, a man in green scrubs was gently shaking him awake.

209

"Mr. Davies, Key Flanerty's awake and asking for you."

Now he remembered. Before dozing off, he'd catalogued the dim light, soothing decorations, and smells of a standard hospital waiting room. But the adrenaline-fueled events in Aggregate still weighed on him.

He shook off grogginess.

"Glad to hear that. And Flora, the other one?"

"Her vitals are fine and she has no injuries, but so far she hasn't awakened. There may be some psychological trauma, so we're keeping her under observation."

Crash followed the doctor down a door-lined corridor. Key occupied one bed in a two-bed room. Her torso was elevated, and a nurse stood by while she drank water through a straw. The nurse nodded, took the glass, and headed for the door.

When the door closed Key spoke.

"It took you so long. Where have you been?"

At first he thought Key was glaring at him, but then he saw concern much like his own in her eyes.

"In the waiting room. This is the first time they've let me see you."

"I thought you'd left."

"I'd never do that…"

He realized what he really wanted to say.

"…not any more. Not ever."

Her eyes searched his, and a tear formed in the corner of one of hers.

She looked down, and when her eyes were visible again, he saw something in them that he had never expected to see: naked vulnerability. He reached for her and gripped her hand. She gripped back. They sat without speaking for several minutes.

Key broke the silence, not the handhold.

"What else have you found out?"

He told her everything. His mind was splintered, part of it still back in the turmoil at Aggregate, part of it wondering about Gary and Suzanne. But mostly he was conscious of an overwhelming realization that Key was going to be all right, and that she wanted him near.

He continued his account on autopilot, increasingly concerned about what might be happening in Lynnwood. He wished he could be two people, one staying here by Key, and the other finding out what was happening to Gary.

From the way Key began to look, he guessed he might have revealed the conflict inside him. She slowly pulled her hand away.

"I'm okay for now, but Gary needs you more. Go on. I'll be waiting to hear from you."

She pulled a phone from under her pillow and held it up.

"Call when you can."

Several messages flickered across her face: determination, doubt, defiance, and need. He felt all those things himself. She must have seen and understood. But a familiar independent and unmovable expression appeared.

"Go."

He was on his way out the door when he remembered that just a few minutes ago he had promised himself never to leave Key. He meant that he would be with her in life, not that he could never leave her side. Did she understand that?

He'd make sure later.

❋ ❋ ❋

The space around Laura was growing more and more claustrophobic. Heavy canvas covered her and limited her movement. Her hands were bound, and each time she moved them she felt the rough surface. Air entered through a small gap. So did wind and rain, and one side of her was wet. Between wind gusts, she heard waves and knew she must be on or near a shore.

She'd been awake when she was bound and blindfolded and forced into the trunk of a car. When the car stopped, someone yanked her out and dragged her across a rough surface, scratching the length of her face. A hand had pulled off her blindfold and a flashlight briefly illuminated the area around her before the canvas cover blocked out everything again.

Now she heard a voice above her, a voice she remembered from the time she was working at Tomson Lake: Grant Tomson. Suddenly the canvas pulled back from around her head and shoulders. Tomson leaned over her, holding a corner. He dropped it, leaving her face uncovered, and took a seat on the nearby table.

"So hello again, Ms. Dickens, and very soon goodbye. We're rounding up your new friend, Gary Seasons. While we wait, let me tell you how very stupid you've been. You can make those your last thoughts."

When she gave no reaction, he went on. His voice rose and words spilled out faster.

"From the moment you started sniffing around the Isadka project, I had you followed. Why? Because Isadka is bigger than just some damn trees. It's part of a plan for new Indian money. The tribes are generating big money now in the casinos. Without guidance, so-called idealists will let them spend it foolishly on schools or hospitals."

Laura couldn't keep quiet.

"You mean things Indians need, rather than what you want."

He snorted a laugh.

"You make my point for me. What they need is economic growth. More than just casinos. Diversification. I know how to create growth, and that requires an end run around stupid regulations. Some Indians see this and work with me."

"And, of course, you and those select few will get rich."

"Why not? Someone has to, or no one will. It's a matter of either leadership or continued servitude. Only a few can be leaders. Might as well be me and those who join me."

"So the white man steps in to help again. Just like the white man knew reservations and resettlement were the best answers for tribal life."

There was enough light to see his expression change. Anger pushed aside arrogance.

"Power and money determine everything. The winners get to make the decisions. The losers don't. Some things never change."

"And of course you'll be the biggest winner."

She knew this conversation was going nowhere, but she was buying time. Not much. She might have detected a hint of doubt in Tomson's voice. Was it possible that he was losing control to something lurking behind him? Something that could lead to mistakes?

Contempt was there now as he waved dismissively.

"Look at where you are. That's all the answer you need."

She kept at it.

"You're no winner. Winners are smart. A real winner would have been able to stay anonymous. It was easy to smoke you out."

Tomson's face contorted, and pushed closer to hers. Manic and ugly all at once. His hand raised, and she tasted real fear.

A high-pitched laugh intruded from the shadows beyond the shelter. Tomson looked at his hand as if it were something alien, and slowly lowered it. Laura could almost feel in her own body the reversal of energy as he reinstalled his public façade.

"Cute, Ms. Dickens. But wrong. As far as the world is concerned, I'm still in the shadows. I've had excellent assistance..."

He pointed toward the shadows.

"...Suzanne has been my eyes and ears. With her on the job, there've been no surprises."

A leggy redhead stepped out, all flounce, a prima donna ready for accolades. Laura aimed her words at what she hoped was the weak link.

"So, Suzanne, the chippy du jour. You must have read stories about what Grant does to his women. Your next stop is the dump."

Suzanne fired back, confident, basking in the moment.

"Wrong, loser. Grant's told me everything about every affair. I like the way he operates, and I'm the one who can make him stronger."

Tomson pushed away the side show and became the unmistakable CEO again.

"Enough distraction. Suzanne has already arranged for the others to be disposed of. They'll have an unfortunate accident that can't be connected to what will happen to you and Gary in just a few minutes."

Laura couldn't control herself.

"Gary?

213

"Hog tied and ready. And Clif trailered his boat up I-5. When the tide shifts, Clif'll tow that little boat out into the Sound, with no life preservers or oars. Just what you'd expect from a careless sailor. He'll set it adrift, first throwing you two overboard, making sure you begin your journey with lungs full of water. Your bodies will sink, then drift who knows where. The boat will eventually wash up somewhere in the Sound. Media will report the sad story of amateur sailors being out in weather they should have avoided. You can wrack your brains for a way out, but the game is already all over. And so's this conversation."

Tomson turned away and stepped into the rain and darkness.

❋ ❋ ❋

Crash could just make out voices behind the side door at Long-cart Motors. It was approaching midnight. He knocked again, this time louder.

The door opened a crack, his view through the narrow vertical space blocked by a body dressed in khaki. The back-lit open sliver of space revealed one eye, dark hair above it and compressed lips below. The lips opened.

"This place is closed."

The door started to shut. Desperation opened Crash's mouth and raised his voice.

"Gotta talk to Officer McHugh."

The voice of the man inside was barely audible.

"Guy says he has to speak to McHugh."

A moment later, the door jerked open and a man exited so quickly that it was impossible to see what was going on inside. He was dressed in jeans and a Central Washington sweatshirt, the letters of which were about level with Crash's eyes. Crash looked up into a broad face, dark eyes, and closely cropped black hair. The man's size dominated all other impressions. He was as tall as Gary but felt twice as broad. Powerful arms hung beside a massive chest—a pair of cannons, locked and loaded.

The man waited for him to start.

"Officer Bill McHugh?"

"And you are?"

"Crash Davies. I was with Gary Seasons until about an hour ago."

The chest and arms relaxed.

"Yeah. I'm McHugh, and Gary told me some about you. He also told me what happened in Aggregate. Hope the two women are okay."

"They're at the hospital. Is Gary here?"

"Seems to have left."

"Did Gary ever mention Suzanne Bickers, that she was at Aggregate, but left?"

"Yeah, he did."

Man, this guy had no gear but gruff.

"Grant Tomson?"

McHugh's tone turned grim.

"Yeah, him, too. That's all I can tell you. Gotta get back inside. We're quizzing Curt Longcart."

"Can I come in?"

McHugh hesitated and Crash rushed on.

"I heard and saw things in Aggregate. Might be relevant to what Longcart says."

McHugh mulled, then held up a hand.

"Wait. I'll see what the locals say. I'm only an observer."

He went back inside. Crash waited, expecting a no-go, but the door opened again and McHugh motioned him inside.

Crash had seen Longcart many times on TV, mostly because you couldn't avoid seeing him. That TV personage was usually spewing enthusiasm, but the man in front of him was hunched, looking a lot older without makeup and the forgiving effects of stage lighting. Mostly, though, Longcart looked cornered, on the verge of bolting or collapsing.

No one noticed when Crash took the seat McHugh pointed at. A younger local policeman was taking the lead, asking about Suzanne Bickers. Longcart fidgeted through a question about what Suzanne actually did for him and, before the question was finished, broke in.

"Look, you're asking about a low level part of our advertising and a person not in my employ. I only know what you know about her, that

215

she makes commercials for Longcart Motors on contract with a PR firm we use in Spokane."

Crash knew he'd be taking a chance by intervening, and might get tossed out, but he couldn't help himself.

"That's a lie."

All eyes turned in his direction. He didn't wait for any more reaction.

"First of all, Gary Seasons told me that he'd seen Suzanne here at Longcart Motors many times, and that you and her are tight. Suzanne admitted to me and other people that she harassed bloggers online on direct orders from you. I just came from a crime scene in Aggregate. Suzanne was there and got away; I think she intended to come here. You must have talked to her."

There were several exaggerations in that statement, but it might have shock value. Crash went on.

"Suzanne kidnapped two women. Gary was knifed and might have been killed. You're involved with attempted murder."

The cops hadn't interrupted. They were all focused on Longcart, watching.

Curt raised his hands, as if asking for understanding, and immediately seemed to realize that the conversation had gone beyond that point. Hands dropped to his sides, his shoulders with them. He stayed slumped while the others waited. When he raised his head, he wore a canny expression. He wanted to bargain.

"Okay. You make it in business by cutting corners. I've cut a lot. No harm there. But do it enough, and you get in with people with no limits. The stakes look worth it until it's too late. If I've done anything wrong, it's waiting too long to cut my losses and get away from people like Grant Tomson. You know, a fib or two don't hurt. But planning murder, that's not me. I'll tell you everything, but I want to make sure you treat me right."

No one spoke. Longcart filled the silence with pleading.

"Look at it this way. If I weren't cooperating, you maybe don't get Tomson. You guys owe me…"

The young policeman took over again.

"No promises until you tell us what you've got. Then we'll see."

Longcart had regained some amount of control. You could almost see his mind whirring, like he'd found a toehold on familiar territory.

"My job was to keep the individual parcel owners in line at Isadka Valley, sweet-talking profits, using tribal loyalty if they were Indians, passing out extra cash on occasion. That's all."

Longcart paused and looked around the circle. Stony silence was all he got. He lowered his head for a moment, raised it again and went on. Relief was there, but immediately turned into anger.

"After a while it wasn't worth the risk. Compared to what Tomson was putting together with the big projects, my cut didn't amount to much. But the point—after a while, the only point—was that this was his project. He had to have everything his way."

Longcart had a head of steam now.

"The small changes in his personality got bigger. No more discussions. It was all orders, crazy orders. Threats. He wasn't talking about Isadka anymore. People who stood in his way was all he could see. Told me I had to deliver Dickens and help him capture Gary. I did the first part, with help from Clif Lerman. Felt bad about it, but I had no choice. I could be next. Then when Gary arrived about an hour ago, Suzanne was here and she took over, shot him up. See, I got sucked in, but soon as I saw what Tomson was doing, I got afraid…for my life. Yeah, I had to do some things to protect myself. Who wouldn't? But I'm not the person you want."

The young policeman took a step forward.

"Cut the bullshit. Where did they take Dickens and Seasons?"

Longcart recoiled and started shaking.

"I don't know, I swear I don't. Only thing I picked up: After she shot Gary with a needle, she made a call. She went off to the side and I couldn't hear much. But I did hear 'boat' and 'tide'. That's all I got."

McHugh spoke up.

"If you wanted to put a boat into the water near here, where would you do it?"

217

"There's a little park due west of here. That'd be the closest. Next best would be the park near the ferry landing in Mukilteo, farther north."

McHugh and the two local policemen huddled in the corner and spoke in low voices. They didn't take long.

McHugh motioned Crash over. He pointed at the younger policeman.

"Stevens—he's the primary—will get out an alert to departments in the area, and he'll personally check out the boat landing west of here. The other cop'll handle Longcart. I'm going up to Mukilteo and check out the park. You're free to leave."

Crash had a different idea.

"Take me along. I'll be extra eyes. Extra hands, if you need them. C'mon."

McHugh looked at the wall as if a window were there. Then at his watch.

"Doubtful about the hands part, but eyes I might need. Will you do everything I tell you, no more and no less?"

"Yes."

"Let's get going."

Crash looked at his watch as he rushed to McHugh's car. Almost 15 minutes had passed since he arrived at Longcart Motors. He hoped they still had time.

❋ ❋ ❋

Laura struggled, then went limp, making small movements that she hoped would interfere with efforts to move her. She tried to convince herself that each moment of delay increased the chances that the cavalry would arrive. But a feeling of hopelessness was gaining ground.

Unseen hands removed the tarp and lifted her up onto the top of a picnic table. At first, being able to breathe fresh air was a relief. But that feeling didn't last long. Her only steady company was heavy rain and sudden wind gusts.

After a while, lights emerged from the gloom. Two flashlights. At first she couldn't see who was behind them. But as the beams moved around, she made out Suzanne in the lead, with a slim man behind her. He struggled under a heavy load, holding on to the wrists of a large body slung over one shoulder.

Suzanne spoke.

"Get him up on a table. Come on, Clif, don't be a wuss."

So this was the Clif that Gary had told her about.

He circled a free table and barely got the torso up on it. Suzanne steadied her flashlight as he hoisted up the bound legs.

Laura saw the face, and her heart sank. It was Gary—his arms, like his legs, bound in cloth strips. Clif took a minute to catch his breath, then spoke.

"Gotta keep on schedule or Mr. Big'll get mad. Time to move her."

Laura tried to stay limp, but Clif hauled her up and got a shoulder underneath. He was surprisingly strong for his build. Her head hung down across his chest. She got a strong whiff of sweat and foul breath, but willed herself not to react.

Suzanne lit the way. A bouncing beam flashed over the water's edge, settling briefly on Gary's small sailboat on a trailer. Its wheels were in the water, ready for launching.

Suddenly Laura was in free fall, and hit the ground hard at the base of a tree. Pain shot through her shoulder blade when it connected with a protruding root. She stifled a cry.

Suzanne's light disappeared, and Clif's went on. The beam bounced a few paces toward the boat again. Laura got a glimpse of Clif perched on the trailer tongue.

There was one thing she needed to do if at all possible. It would not help her now, though it might eventually hurt Tomson. That wasn't much, only slightly better than leaving life with a sense of total failure.

The silver cylinder was still in her side pocket. Anybody's guess if it was still running, or whether it had captured Tomson's voice back at the picnic table. She needed a place for it to be discovered, and started talking with only a vague idea to work from.

"I know I'm going to die."

Clif's voice came back, wrapped in a snide laugh. It wasn't very convincing. Maybe he too was nervous.

219

"Can you let me pray first, at least die at peace with God?"

No response. Her heart sank. Maybe Clif hated religion. His pause was becoming a black shroud, when he spoke.

"Pray where you are. No one's stopping you."

"Like this I can't. I need to be on my knees and do it right."

"Do it or don't. I don't give a shit. Just shut up. Keep talking and I'll shut you up for good."

"Shut me up and you'll get nothing but eternal damnation. I can mention you in my prayers, and ask for forgiveness for you."

Clif said nothing. She kept going, and hoped he was changing his mind.

"There's a rope in the boat. I know because I've sailed it. You can tie it around my neck, untie my wrists and ankles, and give me some time a couple of yards away. That's all I ask. Think of your soul, Clif."

Clif was silent, then she saw the flashlight moving around the boat. A few moments later his voice was right behind her head.

"Two minutes."

She felt something pass in front of her face and put pressure on her neck. Immediately afterwards, the cloth ties on her wrists and ankles were loosened.

Her cramped muscles warned her not to try standing, so she pulled up to a kneeling position and crawled around the tree. The beam of light followed her. She went through unfamiliar motions, imitating friends who had made the sign of the cross. Through the rain, the flashlight's illumination added dim visibility to the ground around her. She half turned her head and spoke to the space behind the light.

"Would you grant me one minute alone with my Lord? I'll give your kindness full mention. You'll still be able to hear me."

The light went out, but she felt the rope tighten on her neck.

For the next two minutes, she did her best to appear to be praying, continuing a steady stream of words. The light came back on. At the same time, she reached into her side pocket slowly, turning slightly to keep that side out of the beam of light. She kept up a low mumble while her hand groped in the parka.

Her fingers slipped, numb from being tied up. It seemed to take forever to free the recorder from that pocket. Finally, the small cylinder came out, and she dropped it by the base of the tree, hoping that it would remain beyond stray rays of the flashlight. That was all she could do.

Just in time, too. The noose on her neck gave a jerk, and she fell to her side. Clif's voice was close by her ear.

"Ready for the rest of it now?"

The flashlight wavered, and she caught a dull glint by the tree as Clif tied up her feet again. God, if Clif should see…don't let him notice.

This time her prayer was real.

❀ ❀ ❀

Gary woke to the sound of impenetrable rain and the pain of a massive headache. He was immediately aware of the constraints on his wrists and ankles, and began yanking and pulling to get free. His whole body responded as if he were back in a football pile-up, using all his strength to get loose from a mountainous weight.

Suddenly the surface below him gave way, and he fell. He just had time to tense when a massive jolt stopped his fall. His whole left side screamed in pain. It took a moment to clear his head. Gradually he took in a concrete floor and cross-hatched wooden supports that resolved into the bottom part of a picnic table.

He was too mad to think. This was the first time he'd lost a fight since he was a young kid.

Disorientation was the partner of pain. He had no idea where he was. The table, he slowly realized, was one of those he'd seen often in parks. He was aware of a roof above. Otherwise, there was only pelting rain beyond the open sides. No park would attract visitors on a night like this.

He made one more try to break free. That effort got him nowhere except to provoke a female laugh that went on and on.

Full consciousness was back. A redheaded woman was mimicking his struggle to get free. He recognized her from the Triplet videos.

Beside her stood a grim man who looked like pictures he'd seen of Grant Tomson. The man cut the woman's laugh short and shut down her little act with an impatient wave.

"Enough, Suzanne. Let's finish it. Check around and see we haven't left anything."

With that, Tomson snatched up Gary's legs, grasping them at the knees. He was stronger than he looked. Suzanne grabbed an arm, and the two of them dragged him out into the rain. He struggled, but they maintained control.

Gary had to concentrate on keeping his head elevated a much as possible. It banged a couple of times against the concrete floor of the shelter, and then over what felt like a rock border to the momentary relief of grass beyond. Tomson dropped his legs and flicked on a flashlight, shining it on Laura. Her hands were tied behind her back and a noose hung around her neck. Behind her, Clif held the end of a rope attached to the noose.

There was a moment of eerie silence, then Tomson erupted.

"Goddammit, Clif. I said no ropes. They leave marks. What was there in 'no marks' that you couldn't understand?"

The flashlight shifted to Clif's face. Tomson moved in that direction, and Gary watched his arm descend through the beam of light. There was a loud crunch. The light jiggled, dropped to the ground, and settled on a prone Clif.

Tomson moved in and out of the arc of light as he removed the noose from Laura's neck.

Though Gary's brain told him it was useless, he threw his remaining strength against his bonds. The space in front of his eyes went red, and he imagined his hands on Tomson's neck, watching his eyes bulge in fear. That surge didn't last, as he felt a sharp pain in his left shoulder. The old football injury. The flashlight beam moved toward the water. He heard Suzanne speak but he couldn't make out the words. Someone pointed the beam at a familiar small boat. Tomson and Suzanne grabbed Laura's legs and dragged her toward it. Their figures were ghosts, appearing and disappearing in the dim light, the darkness and the driving rain.

A voice penetrated the incessant beat of the waves and the snare drum of rain. He held his breath so the rasp of his own breathing would stop interfering.

Then came a shrill cry, an anguished "Noooo" from Laura. Then nothing but water sounds again. Gary redoubled his struggle, heaving at his restraints. Pain shot down his left side into his hip. A yowl rose from inside him, lost immediately in the vastness of the night.

Light flared, and he tensed for the arrival of new pain. But this light stayed steady. He opened his eyes to see another flashlight approaching, and heard his name called out.

With what strength remained, he repeated three words over and over: Laura, help, water.

Then he passed out.

❋ ❋ ❋

Crash knelt over Gary. Bill McHugh ran toward the water's edge.

A hand lantern from the police cruiser gave off a wide-angled light. Crash set it on the ground and worked first on the triple-knotted strips of cloth around Gary's ankles. Completely soaked, they allowed no firm grip. He got through the first knot, and the second one went a little faster. At that point, Gary woke up. His eyes swiveled toward the water and back. They were wild with distress.

"Laura. How is she?"

Gary's body convulsed, trying to get up. Crash tried to calm him.

"Take it easy and let me finish untying you and we can both go to…"

A hoarse yell interrupted.

"You go now!"

Crash raised his voice to match.

"Bill McHugh's already down there. Let me finish. Turn on your side."

Tense with reluctance, Gary managed a half-turn that exposed his wrists. When Crash pushed him farther in that direction, Gary stifled a cry of pain.

"Left shoulder and arm messed up."

223

Crash slowed down. He finally got through the last knots on Gary's wrists when a voice penetrated the rain.

"Shine the light over here."

They watched McHugh carefully lower a woman's body to the ground and immediately begin CPR. Gary dragged himself to the woman's side as McHugh alternately forced breath into her mouth and stiff-armed her chest.

Crash could do nothing but watch and hold the light. The rain was letting up a bit. His attention shifted when he heard voices, then saw three figures approaching. As they entered the circle of light, he noticed two police uniforms. It took him longer to recognize the third person—smaller, red hair plastered down. Suzanne.

McHugh rose and looked at Crash.

"You take over. Here, I'll show you. I'll be right back."

Crash watched carefully and went on with the CPR. Gary, crouching in pain, took a position at his side. In a hoarse voice, he encouraged and gave tips.

"You're doing fine. Slow down your compression and give more time between reps. I wish I could take over. But my arm…"

McHugh conferred with the two other policemen and then disappeared into the gloom with one of them.

Less than a minute later, McHugh returned with a man's body slung over one shoulder. He didn't bother to lean over, just dropped the body. It didn't move when it hit the ground with a slushy thud.

Immediately McHugh moved back beside Laura and took over again. Gary knelt in close by Laura's other side. Laura was on her stomach now, McHugh straddling her waist, leaning his straight arms onto her rib cage, releasing and repeating.

They waited in numb silence as the seconds ticked by with no response from Laura. Crash was sure that she was gone, despite the way McHugh kept up his rhythm. So he wasn't prepared when Laura's back heaved. She choked and began coughing; water ran out of her open mouth. The coughing went on, gradually subsiding. A few minutes later, she was sitting up, dazed and silent, but alive. Gary moved in closer, gently draping his good arm over her shoulders.

Laura tried to speak, and gagged.

Gary calmed her.

"Wait, we have time now."

Her head came up shaking.

"Get...recorder. By...tree."

Crash moved to follow her instruction. He turned on his phone flashlight and walked over to the nearest tree, where he spotted a shiny object—a cylinder about three inches long—and picked it up.

On the cylinder's front, an LED readout indicated it was just before midnight on November 30. Crash had trouble fitting that information into any context—it was as if everything that had just happened occurred in a special, separate time, unrelated to normal dates.

Before he could take another step, McHugh was beside him.

"I'll take that."

Crash handed the recorder to McHugh and simultaneously his phone buzzed. At that moment he was distracted by the sound of vehicles approaching and the glare of their headlights, and had to move out of the way.

When he returned his attention to his phone, the buzzing had stopped.

DECEMBER 1

Key watched the second hand reach Roman numeral XII and circle beyond it. It was now after midnight on the first of December. Raindrops pelted the double-pane hospital windows hard enough that she could hear them.

Every few minutes for the last two hours, she'd looked at the face of that big clock on the wall. Yesterday, today, it didn't matter. Her mind was still thrashing, and she'd lost hold on what previously had seemed simple and obvious.

Since Crash left, she'd hardly moved. Now she was wide awake after dozing for less than an hour, haunted by worries. He'd been gone more than two hours. Lynnwood was not that far away. He should have called by now.

Well, maybe not. Maybe things were happening, and he couldn't call. If it had taken this long, maybe it meant bad news.

She tried to concentrate on the good news the doctor had given her. Flora had briefly returned to consciousness and asked for water before she sank away again. The fact that she had been able to speak at all was good.

Key was starting to doze off again when her phone startled her. She fumbled for it, tapped on, and heard Crash's voice, finally.

"I'm okay. Things are under control. Lots is happening, so I couldn't make a call before now."

"Tell me.

"Well, it's raining hard here and the place is tough to find, but really bad stuff…"

Crash began the way he often did, from where he was in the moment, and went backwards. She lost track that way.

"Start at the beginning."

"Yeah, okay. Don't have much time."

"Quick, then. The basics."

Crash filled her in on the trip to Lynnwood, Curt's confession, and his mad dash to Mukilteo with McHugh.

"We got there just in time. They were drowning Laura, and Gary was next. I actually thought Laura was done for, but McHugh did CPR

229

in time. The police are here now and they're telling me to hang up. Gotta go. How's Flora?"

"Better. Call when you can. Go."

Key finally realized how hard she had been gripping the now-silent phone. The knot in her stomach was still there. She tried to stand but sank back down.

So Crash had called and he was okay and they'd talked. But where did that leave her—and him?

God, she was tired. Key moved to the rumpled sheets on top of her bed. Prone and waiting for sleep, her troubling thoughts gradually got dimmer until unconsciousness seeped in.

Just before darkness descended, she thought once more about Crash, glad he was okay. Why didn't she feel complete relief? They should talk. Or was she already thinking beyond that?

✻ ✻ ✻

Laura began to understand where she was: strapped to a stretcher-like pad. By leaning her head to the side and looking down, she spotted wheels. So she must be on a portable gurney. Gary sat on a nearby table—a picnic table, in some kind of shelter. It reminded her of a place she'd been, maybe ages ago. Her staggered mind said something huge had happened. But so far the fragments didn't fit together into a whole reality.

Her body told her more than her brain could. Her throat was sandpaper-sore. Her chest felt as if giant forceps had pried her ribcage open, while a pair of relentless pile drivers pummeled her back.

Every thought was full of water. Lots of water—impending, scary water. Maybe the man in uniform could help. He was talking, speaking to a body that lay on the next table. That was curious.

She heard her name. When it came a second time, she realized that the man in uniform was talking to her. She tried words.

"That's me."

That was all she could manage. Sleep. She needed to sleep. Sleep would help her, even if nothing else could.

230

❄ ❄ ❄

The lights in the picnic shelter were now fully on. In their glow, Crash had seen two EMTs moving a body on a gurney. Clif Lerman, McHugh told him.

More people entered the picture. A man Crash didn't recognize lay prone on top of another table, either unconscious or pretending to be. A few feet away from him, a policeman stood by Suzanne.

Then an older officer arrived, wearing an attitude of authority. In a low voice, he conferred with the officer beside Suzanne. Perched nearby, close enough to hear what was going on, Bill McHugh was paying attention.

Suzanne had been sullen and silent. Now she yelled.

"I gotta pee."

The senior officer spoke, loud enough so Suzanne could not fail to hear.

"Give her two minutes inside, no more. If she's not out by then, go in and get her."

The junior man led Suzanne out into the rain. As soon as she was out of earshot, the prone man rose to a half-sitting position and spoke.

"Thank you for coming to our rescue, officer. I assume you're in charge. May I ask your name?"

The barrel-chested older officer eyed the speaker for a long moment.

"Would you identify yourself."

It was a command, not a question.

The man on the table glared, but then adjusted to neutral cooperation.

"Grant Tomson."

So this was the famous Grant Tomson. Crash had been around a few well-known individuals in the past; usually their actual appearance surprised him in some way. He hadn't imagined a specific image of Tomson, but this man, even though caught in unusual circumstances, exuded the in-your-face arrogance of his advance notices.

"Thank you. I'm Edgar Zelko, Chief of Police, Mukilteo."

231

Tomson pulled himself farther up and swung his legs toward the floor. His voice switched to fawning respect.

"No, thank *you*, Chief Zelko. You and your men got here just in time. The young lady, Ms. Bickers, has been acting erratically and so has the young man who was with her, Clif Lerman. I overheard them talking about a plan to 'take care of' Gary Seasons. I was concerned and decided to follow them here. I found them dragging Seasons toward the water, and I managed to overcome Lerman. I was just going to the rescue of the woman over there…"

He pointed at Laura.

"…when Ms. Bickers hit me from behind."

Zelko showed no reaction.

"And how do you know Lerman and Bickers?"

"Lerman has worked for Curt Longcart of Longcart Motors. I've had a minor business relationship with Longcart, and he recommended Lerman to me. I used him occasionally as a messenger. I saw Bickers several times with Lerman and knew her name. Nothing more."

Crash felt hot anger rise inside him. Tomson was lying. McHugh must be furious too, but was showing no emotion.

Zelko nodded and bored in.

"So you heard something that might indicate intent to commit a crime. But you didn't call the police? Why was that?"

A note of pride slipped into Tomson's voice.

"I'm a responsible citizen. I know how busy and overworked law enforcement is. I didn't want to send valuable civic resources on a wild goose chase. I knew Bickers has a vivid imagination, so there might have been considerable distance between stated intent and actuality. I thought it would be enough to follow Lerman and Bickers and call the police right away if it turned out to be dangerous."

Crash saw something move in the rim of light around the enclosure. The younger policemen and Suzanne had returned. How much had they heard?

The chief went on, raising his voice.

"I thought you said you had only briefly seen Suzanne Bickers. How could you know she had a 'vivid imagination'?"

232

"Certainly observant of you to remember that. I developed that impression when I overheard her talking to Lerman."

"So your claim is that you were here only to rescue individuals from an action planned and carried out by Lerman and Bickers?"

"Exactly."

A high-pitched female voice shouted out.

"Liar!"

Everyone turned toward Suzanne. She stepped forward to the edge of the enclosure, pointing a shaking finger.

Tomson swiveled his gaze back to Zelko.

"Prepare yourself for an imaginary reconstruction of events. I don't believe Ms. Bickers has a firm grasp on reality."

Zelko kept his eyes on Suzanne.

"What is it you'd like to say?"

"He's throwing me under the bus. I can't believe it. For months he's used me, fucked me, planned all this. And now he blames..."

Tomson stared straight at Zelko, raising his voice to speak over Suzanne.

"Right away she demonstrates my case. If you haven't noticed already, Ms. Bickers has an overdeveloped gift for the dramatic. Here is someone I helped, now turning against me. I pity her, but I must defend myself against her lies."

Condescension crept into Tomson's interjection. Did Zelko and McHugh hear that, too?

Suzanne took a deep breath and spoke again, switching to an unnaturally calm voice, so soft that Crash had to strain to hear her.

"He had a gun."

All movement stopped. Zelko broke the silence.

"Would you repeat that?"

"Grant had a gun. I don't know where it is now. I think he tossed it in the water..."

Tomson interrupted.

"I have to protest this libel."

233

Zelko waved him off and instructed the junior officer to search the area near the sailboat and in the water, if necessary. Then he returned his attention to Tomson.

"Protest noted. You'll have another chance back at the station. For now, do you have anything to add?"

Tomson straightened to a stance that was both authoritative and at ease: a man confident that he was back in charge, or soon would be.

"I was glad to offer the full facts until Ms. Bickers began her unfounded accusations. From this point on, I choose to delay my comments until I am with legal counsel."

Crash saw where all of this was going, and a chill cooled his rising hope that Tomson would be punished. If the man was always so calculating, Suzanne might not be able to prove that there had been anything between them other than professional contact. Tomson could stand by his flimsy reasons for being here at the scene. He'd claim a gun was for self-protection.

And he might actually get away with it. Longcart might crack and Clif, if he survived, might testify against him. But right now, Tomson could be slipping through their fingers.

Into that rising gloom, Bill McHugh spoke up.

"If it's okay with you, Zelko, I'd like to be present during the formal interrogation. This case may tie in with Mr. Tomson's former brush with the law."

McHugh had been there all along, standing back in the shadows. When he spoke, he took a step into the circle of light and looked directly at Tomson.

At first, Tomson met McHugh's challenge, his arrogant expression unchanged. Then, for an instant, his eyes fell and Crash felt a small uptick of hope.

✳ ✳ ✳

"Let's go over your statement one more time, Mr. Tomson."

At the Mukilteo station, Gary noticed a deceptive patience in Chief Zelko's continuing interrogation. Bill McHugh, when he spoke, used the same tone.

Tomson no longer bothered to hide his bored arrogance. This interview was little more than a nuisance for him, and he seemed to enjoy showing it. His lawyer, an unshaven man in slacks and a pullover, was waiting for them at the station when they arrived around 3 am.

Gary sat with Laura in a small space off the interview room, able to see what was going on through a one-way mirror and to hear the conversation over a loudspeaker. He and Laura had not had a chance to talk alone since they left the park. After the events in Mukilteo, EMTs had taken her to a hospital for examination, and the doctor had concluded that she was up to giving a statement to the police. She'd finished that about half an hour ago. She was pale and withdrawn, and occasionally dozed. But for the most part, she seemed aware of what was being said in the interview.

Tomson was repeating what Gary had already heard, but Laura was hearing it for the first time.

"As I've said several times already, I'm a businessman, and I pay close attention to the performance of my staff. What they do outside of their responsibilities as employees is up to them."

Chief Zelko and McHugh waited. Tomson glanced at his lawyer, got a nod in return, and went on.

"So my acquaintance with Ms. Bickers and Mr. Lerman was extremely limited. She worked for a public relations firm in Spokane—Curry and Edson, which does work for me. I've met Ms. Bickers on, perhaps, four occasions, either in Spokane or Shoreline. Frankly, I couldn't tell you exactly."

McHugh interrupted.

"You've never met her alone in personal circumstances?"

Tomson smiled and raised a hand, palm toward McHugh.

"Please. That's not allowable in my book, and I find the image of my having a relationship with such a young lady rather ludicrous."

The lawyer leaned over and whispered to Tomson. Tomson's curt nod flashed irritation.

"Counsel tells me not to volunteer information. But I'm trying to be helpful."

Gary realized that Suzanne wasn't the only one around who could put on a convincing act.

Zelko prompted further.

"Let's talk about Lerman."

Tomson tried a serious expression.

"How is Clif, by the way? I felt I had to subdue him, but I never intended serious harm."

Zelko waved him off.

"He's under medical care. Now, explain your prior relationship with him."

"There you have me, and I'm not proud of it. I've used Mr. Lerman as a deliveryman on several occasions. I did so at first on Longcart's recommendation and, honestly, was not pleased with Lerman's dependability. But by that time I'd learned something about the young man's difficult background, and I kept him on. I've always been sympathetic to those who need a break."

Zelko nodded.

"We may return to that, but let's continue. Did those limited contacts lead to your being at Mukilteo Park last night?"

Tomson adjusted his position, sitting straighter, with his hands clasped in front of him on the table.

"I mentioned that I had business dealings with Curt Longcart. Infrequent and unprofitable ones, but Longcart has connections with Indian tribes that represent promising partnerships for the future. For that reason I may have granted Longcart more leeway than was wise. I regret that."

Tomson put on a rueful look and, getting no reaction, went on.

"Longcart leaned hard on me to back a consortium of small landholders near the Isadka Valley logging site. The idea was that those owners would each apply for a small-parcel variance, which would allow them each to log a higher percentage of land than if the parcels were bundled together. Then Longcart would organize them into a single enterprise. That would give the owners the same economies of scale as a large company, but they'd also be able to log more land."

McHugh interjected.

"Wouldn't that be illegal?"

Tomson sat up straighter.

"Of course. I saw that immediately and refused to cooperate in such a scheme."

Zelko took over.

"Let me get this straight. You were given a chance to get involved in a possibly illegal scheme. You said no, which presumably took you out of the loop. But then you showed up at Mukilteo. How did you know to be there if you were no longer part of the group?"

Tomson wasn't fazed in the least.

"I can see how you would find that puzzling. But there is an explanation."

"Go on."

"Coincidence. I, too, thought I was done with Isadka Valley, with Suzanne Bickers and Clif Lerman. But I wasn't finished with Curt Longcart. He called me to ask for a meeting. He didn't say what it was about. Since I've invested in Curt's ventures over the years, and he in mine, I thought I ought to find out. We met at Longcart Motors."

He paused as if consulting his memory. Zelko prodded again.

"Okay, you're there at Longcart Motors. Then what?"

Tomson's lawyer leaned over again. Tomson listened briefly, shrugged, and turned back to Zelko.

"Council advises caution again. But I'm a busy man, and would rather get this done with. We all have more important things to do. We began our discussion in the conference room at Longcart Motors."

"Time?"

For the first time, Tomson hesitated. It was only a hiccup, but it was there.

"Exact time? I couldn't say for sure. The events of last night are still a blur. We met last evening. I'd finished dinner and was returning home."

"To downtown Seattle?"

"I'm temporarily residing elsewhere."

"Where?"

Tomson glanced at his lawyer.

"I fail to see how that is relevant."

Zelko's voice stayed level, but with added weight.

"We'll be the ones to decide what's relevant. But go on."

"Very well. I met Longcart sometime around 9 pm. An unusual time, I admit, but his office was on my way. Longcart made one more try to convince me to back the Isadka project. I refused again. He persisted, and I ended our discussion."

"And then? Are you going to tell us how you ended up in Mukilteo?"

"I'm getting to that if you'll be patient."

Condescension crept into his voice. Zelko and McHugh didn't change their unreadable expressions. Tomson returned immediately to his cooperative act.

"Longcart was angry and left through a rear door, slamming it behind him. On my way out, I visited the restroom next to the conference room, leaving the door slightly ajar. I'd finished and turned off the light when I heard a door open and close and then the voices of, first Lerman, then Longcart. I stayed quiet, not sure what to do. I didn't intend to listen, but when I grasped the nature of the conversation, I was stunned."

"Why was that?"

Tomson looked down. When he raised his face, it was properly serious.

"I didn't get all of it. But it was clear that Longcart was holding two people, and that they had something to do with the Isadka venture. Longcart ordered Clif to 'handle' them. That's the word he used, 'handle', but I knew it meant 'kill'. I felt I had to do something."

"So what did you do?"

"I followed them to a van where Longcart, Clif, and Suzanne loaded a body into the van. I couldn't see who it was. Longcart went back to the dealership. Suzanne and Clif stood by the van arguing in low voices. I couldn't hear anything because of the rain, but Clif appeared to be resisting. Eventually, they got into the van and drove off."

"Then what did you do?"

"The only thing I could think to do at the time; I got in my car and followed them."

238

"You didn't think of calling the police?"

"Of course I did."

"Then why didn't you?"

"Chief Zelko, put yourself in my position. If I'd called, it would have taken time. Visibility was terrible. If I didn't follow the van immediately, I would lose it, and once I was driving, I had to concentrate on the road and the vehicle ahead. There was never a moment when I thought I could safely use my phone. Once we arrived at Mukilteo I did try, but there was no connectivity."

Zelko gave no indication whether he accepted this response as adequate or not.

"So your statement is that, aside from your conversation with Longcart, you had no other conversations that evening either in person or by phone with Bickers or Lerman?"

Tomson hesitated.

"I was caught in a confusing and rapidly changing situation. I'm giving you my best recollection. It's possible that I may remember other details."

Zelko nodded.

"Fine. Let's have a brief break and, when we come back, take up the matter of the gun."

❋ ❋ ❋

"You sure you're up to this?"

The officer who introduced himself as Larry Henry asked the question with professionally flat courtesy. Laura couldn't tell whether he was testing her recall or offering her a solicitous way to delay the interview. It didn't matter. She wanted to get her side of the story into the record, even with her lingering headache.

"I'm fine."

"Let's start with how you got to Mukilteo."

Adding as many details as she could remember, she took the officer through the call from Longcart, their dinner meeting, and the assault that left her trapped in the trunk of a car.

"Can you identify or describe your assailant?"

239

"It was so sudden, and so dark, that I couldn't get a look at the guy who grabbed me, but Longcart called him 'Clif'. I didn't actually see him until Mukilteo."

"That would be Clif Lerman?"

"I assume so. I only learned his last name last night. But the man addressed as Clif did attack me."

"Was there any indication why he attacked you?"

"From the beginning, he was following Longcart's orders. In Mukilteo, he took orders from Grant Tomson, too."

"Do you know why they wanted to attack you?"

"Because I was investigating the logging project at Isadka Valley, and they didn't want anyone nosing around. Two of us, Gary Seasons and I, found out that the project might have been presented to state agencies as something it wasn't. Longcart and Tomson were behind the whole thing. They didn't want anyone blowing the whistle."

"So what happened at Mukilteo?"

She heard a quiver in her voice as she told him about her conversation with Tomson and the plan to drown her and Gary.

"Go on."

"Clif carried me down near the boat. I pretended I needed to pray and dumped a voice recorder by a tree. Officer McHugh has it now."

"Yes, I know about the recorder. We'll come back to that, but what happened to you then?"

"Tomson was mad at Clif for using a rope on my neck. I couldn't really see, but I heard a hard cracking sound. After that, I didn't hear Clif anymore. I tried to fight, but Tomson got me into the water and pushed my head under. I held out as long as I could…"

Laura felt herself trembling and had to stop. After a moment, she realized she was holding her breath. Slowly she let it out until her lungs were empty, then inhaled sharply. The terror of being back there in the water receded enough that she could continue.

"After that I have no memory until I came to."

She wracked her brain for more, but all that occurred was a question.

"The voice recorder, do you have it?"

"Chief Zelko does."

"Did it work?"

"You bet. Pretty sweet little device. It's all there—Tomson talking, and the exchange with Clif before he hit him. The sound of the blow to Clif's head is faint, but it's there."

The questioning stopped. Good timing. Her body slumped, and she knew she was done in more ways than one.

❊ ❊ ❊

"That fucker's not going to get away with it."

Crash watched through the one-way mirror as McHugh interviewed Suzanne. She was digging deep into her bag of theatrical tricks, delivering each statement with over-the-top emphasis or quiet, heart-rending pleas of innocence. McHugh had her figured out from the get-go, giving her free rein for her act, always using the same flat voice for his questions. They'd been at it for half an hour.

"Is it your contention, then, that Tomson forced you to be involved in his schemes?"

"Absolutely."

"How did he force you?"

"First he promised to help me get a raise with Longcart. The old man's stingy beyond belief. Do you have any idea what it's like to live at the poverty line? Society has no respect for actors."

"Nothing in your statement describes force."

She flared.

"Grant knows how to get what he wants. He gave me small amounts of money, promising a large pay-off later. Despite my resistance, he forced me into a sexual relationship."

"He raped you?"

"What's the difference? More like he made it clear that all his promises depended on my having sex with him."

"How long have you been providing that?"

"About six months."

"And during all that time, you found no way to walk away from his demands?"

241

Her voice rose in anguish.

"There's no way you can understand. By that time, I knew what he did to people who crossed him. Besides, I'd spent money on an apartment, clothes, better recording equipment for the Triplets. I couldn't face the debt. He had me in his control."

"Did you ever think of involving the police?"

Anguish slid into thinly disguised contempt.

"Puleeze. My word versus Grant Tomson's. Gimme a break."

She seemed to realize she'd gone too far. She stopped and regrouped.

"You know, I don't like how this has gone. I made mistakes, yeah. But I didn't have any idea that murder would be involved. I would have run away screaming if he told me that. I'll cooperate all you need. The guy's a scheming, using bastard and my only crime is in not seeing that sooner."

McHugh reached forward to turn off a recording device.

"We'll see. Thank you for your cooperation, Ms. Bickers."

Crash stayed where he was until Suzanne was led from the interview room. McHugh gathered papers into a thin file and rose to leave.

In the hallway, Crash caught up with him.

"So have we got enough to convict?"

McHugh shrugged and kept on walking.

"Only the DA can answer that. No 'we' about it."

He stopped and smiled.

"Look, I didn't mean to blow you off. We wouldn't be here if you hadn't put out an alert. You helped us get this far. I want to thank you."

His smile faded and immediately he became again an inscrutable weapon of the law.

"Not my favorite part of the process, all dancing and waiting. How about a cup of coffee?"

DECEMBER 9

"Nice place you've got here."

Gary watched Laura. He followed her eyes as they scanned his living room. How could he not have noticed they weren't blue, but more like aqua? No chance that he'd forget that color again.

When they'd finally found an opportunity to talk, just the two of them, his house seemed as good a place as any. And, he had to admit, he wanted her to see it.

In the post-Seahawk days, when he was flush with cash, he'd mostly made acceptable financial decisions. The bad ones he regretted; but among the good ones, his best had been to buy this house. Many of the guys, especially the superstars, built or bought humongous places in rich suburbs. He didn't know where the instinct came from to get something completely different. In retrospect, he'd been lucky.

For one thing, a modest craftsman house didn't cost him an arm and a leg to maintain. For another, he'd bought the place with all the furniture of longtime previous owners; and the more he lived with those pieces, the more he liked them. Apparently, Laura did too.

"This living room feels familiar. You used to see more like it, so much wood and that hand-crafted feel."

There was room for her beside him on the settee, but she'd chosen the chair opposite.

"It's the real thing. Whatever wasn't made by a furniture-maker was made by the owner. He and his wife lived here for over fifty years. I got his shop behind the garage, too. No time to use it much now, but I intend to."

"Missionary style, is that it? Kinda boxy."

"I think that's right. All I know is it suits me."

He thought back to their last brief conversation on his sailboat. They were treading water again. Maybe neither one of them was good at starting the personal stuff.

"How are you feeling?"

She let out a low laugh.

"Same as I said on the phone. Physically, almost back to normal. I can't shake a kind of spacy feeling, and my dreams are bad. Otherwise, no change. And you?"

"I haven't forgotten what happened. But I've also been thinking beyond that."

"Beyond?"

He was hopeful she could guess what he meant, but at the same time he was reluctant to go there. Deeper water surrounded them. He didn't even know how to start.

She beat him to it.

"I want to say something before I forget it. I want to thank you for helping me start to find an answer to a question that's been bothering me. I can do things, and I've done them—you know, rowing, academics. But I never felt a sense of purpose. I thought purpose had to be there before you decided you wanted to commit to something. Now I know I had it wrong. You jump in and do, and then figure out whether to go on or do something different. At least that's the way it works for me."

She paused. Her eyes roamed and he saw her searching for words.

"These last weeks have been horrible in some ways. They've left me more wary. But I've also lost my tentativeness. I see now why trees and forestry and even dry things like regulations are worth investing your life in. I don't know how long that feeling will last, but it's there now. And you know what's a big part of that realization?"

"No, what?"

"Watching you and the way you operate. I see how your heritage and, I guess, where you grew up have given you a connection with the environment. I want that for myself. I want to reach the comfort level you have with life. I need that comfort if those other abstractions—goals, purpose, you know—are ever going to have real meaning. So I've decided to stick with Natural Resources and concentrate more on the long-range importance of the work. I hope you can go on helping with that."

He was touched, encouraged, and—what?—impelled to laugh. Which he did, immediately regretted it, and quickly got serious.

"Yeah, I laughed because what you described is too…what'll I call it? Idealized? Anyway, it's not what I've been, most of my life. No way can I be your model. Not if you really know me. I've been distant from my heritage. I lived in the woods, then, abandoned the forest for stadiums. I sold out to money and just barely caught myself before I sold out all the way. I posed as a downtrodden Indian who played on white guilt to advance myself. Some role model."

It felt good to get that all out.

Laura still sat where she was. She hadn't recoiled in shock. In fact, she wore a look of surprise. What was it that he'd thought earlier? About diving into deep water. They were in it already. So he leaned toward her and plunged all the way in.

"I have dreams, too, and they've been about you in trouble and my not being able to help."

She followed him into the current.

"I know you did all you could. It was my fault that I didn't tell you sooner about meeting Longcart."

"Why didn't you?"

"I've puzzled over that. It's complicated. Partly, I didn't want to pull you into something you'd rather avoid. But I think, looking back on it, I needed to test myself. Prove I could handle a tough situation. Rowing taught me how to do that in one kind of situation, but I wasn't confident about others. I had to find out on my own, like I always have."

He understood, but hoped there was more. He scratched his chin, trying to look thoughtful as he bought time. Oh hell. Just say it.

"Could you also have been running away from me? Part of so many things I've done, since I met you, I've done with you in mind. I didn't even realize that at first, but now I can see it. I wondered if we had met casually, no job pressures and not so much baggage, if we'd… you know, be closer now."

She didn't move but all of a sudden seemed further away. His heart started to sag. Then she spoke.

"Hooked up? Be lovers by now?"

247

Her eyes were down, like she was talking more to herself than to him. When she raised her eyes, he expected distance but saw affection instead. A tentative smile appeared.

"Don't think I didn't think about that. A lot. But we were always running off doing things, and no moment was right. When I started to recuperate, I thought about you. I'm really attracted to you. But the better I got, the more something else intruded."

Feelings of excitement and calm entered him simultaneously. He'd thought only of together or not—yes or no—and lived with the rising pressure of a fateful moment. Her body language and her words told him of a different way. He couldn't see it yet, but he wanted to know what she meant. She began again.

"Neither of us really knows who the other is."

"You mean like being white and Indian?"

"Other things, too, like what we want out of life."

This time she was the one who laughed.

"God, how serious! Of course, if we go there, I'd have to ask you about your football groupies."

He fumbled for something to say. She continued before he could form a response.

"I had a few boyfriends that I got close to. One after high school and one rower from Berkeley, in particular."

"You didn't have to tell me that. I'm interested in everything about you. But it doesn't change how I feel about you."

"And how do you feel?"

A real conversation began: formless on the surface but shaped by a willingness to learn. Back in time, then forward to the recent past. She was the fearless one at first, and he dared gradually to match her. They moved to different places in the room, then outside, where fast moving clouds gave them temporary glimpses of blue sky. Two hours later they sat across from each other in the kitchen, with their half-eaten salads on table mats in front of them.

Laura played with her fork. Gary spoke.

"I want to go on seeing you. You got it right about needing to know more about each other. Today's a good start, so let's stick with what works and just see what the future brings."

She nodded.

"That feels right. And I agree…"

Then a shy smile showed up.

"As much as I can. But the attraction was real, and it hasn't gone away."

"You're not the only one. Just so you know."

They finished their salads in a tantalizing silence and were doing the dishes together when Gary extended an earlier part of their conversation.

"Did it ever occur to you how much we may have contributed to what happened to us?"

She looked up. Startled, then only puzzled.

"How?"

"Think of it this way: Isadka was never proven to be another potential Gideon, we just assumed it might be. Nothing wrong with that, but we kept building up that possibility until it seemed like a probability. Why? I thought I needed to demonstrate my competence to OPUS. Maybe you felt the same way about Natural Resources. So we dug deeper. Longcart and, especially, Tomson worried that reminders of Gideon would lead to a no-go at Isadka. The more we pushed for information, the more they thought they had to deal with us. We scared them. So we ended up at Mukilteo."

Laura reacted.

"Our information was better than what our bosses had. Like what I got from Rick Groff, you got from Jeff Winter, and we both did from Longcart."

She went quiet, thinking. Her bowed head came up and she looked at him.

"But you're right. We took some information too much at face value. On the other hand, we acted. We got the situation moving."

Gary smiled.

"Right. And because we acted, we got involved with Key. Tomson upped the ante on getting her tape when he thought it was a real danger to his plans. He might have found her anyway. We made misjudgments, okay, but because we got involved we may have saved Key's life."

"Pretty far out."

He reflected, added a chuckle.

"Unintended consequences aren't always bad, huh? And we did get to know each other. We've got a new way of checking reality."

A smile appeared, as she moved to the towel rack.

"I'd say we did pretty well on part one."

He reached for her.

"Do you really want to wait for part two to start itself?"

The towel fell to the floor.

DECEMBER 10

Crash sipped his morning coffee, sitting by himself in Key's basement. There was a difference between his surroundings now and how he remembered them. He couldn't define its importance yet.

In one corner was a neat stack of boxes that wouldn't have drawn any outsider's attention. In his mind, it was a mountain, containing his significant possessions: his computer, a small number of books he would never part with. And one change of clothes.

The pile had a voice, too, reminding him that they couldn't wait any longer to talk about issue number one. What, honestly, was happening between them? Nothing had been clarified since Mukilteo.

Tired as he was when he was released, he'd accepted a ride to Lynnwood, picked up his car from the lot at Longcart Motors, and driven to the hospital, where Key was waiting for him in the visitors' lounge.

He had hoped she might to come to him with a hug; but no, she kept her distance. She told him that Flora, once released, would be staying with her for another couple of days, at least.

She glanced at him.

"Then we'll see."

See? What did that mean?

He had a lot of things he wanted to talk about, but hadn't dared to bring them up until he got some sense of what Key wanted. Much as it hurt to stay silent, he realized he shouldn't push her, so he said goodbye and drove back to Seattle.

There he went back to work, but almost immediately decided that he didn't want to continue at the glass studio; it just didn't mean that much anymore. The spark of interest that drove his choices was gone. Two days after restarting, he gave his notice.

His reasons for continuing as a watchman at the construction business also collapsed. When he told the owner he was not likely to stay on much longer, the man angrily told him he had one hour to clear out his things. He called Key to tell her what had happened.

To his surprise, she offered to let him move some stuff to her place "for a while, until things get sorted out." Everything else was in his car, parked on a side street two blocks away. Last night they'd politely agreed they were both tired, and Key had gone upstairs to sleep.

Now the basement door opened, and there she was.

"I've been talking with Flora. She says she has to make a choice, and just sitting around here doesn't work for her anymore. She either goes home and stays or finds some reason that keeps her in Seattle. We talked about her going to a community college."

She stayed motionless at the doorway.

"Sounds like a good plan."

He tried to match Key's casual tone, but that seemed to irritate her.

"Yeah, but for what? It's not that easy. How long does she stay here? What will she do?"

"C'mon. Sit down. Sounds like there's a lot to consider."

Key strode to the sofa and sat, arms crossed. Crash dropped his voice a notch.

"Does she have any ideas?"

"One. She says the time here has been good for her. She has friends who she thinks might be different if they could get away from the worst parts of rez life. Not forever, but long enough to see that something different is possible. She wants to go back eventually, but she'd like to get some training here first."

"Okay, and how would she do that?"

Gradually, Key was relaxing.

"I know it sounds crazy, but she wants to use this house. Suppose it was fixed up so that people like her could stay for a few weeks, maybe even months. With some alterations, six, maybe eight more could stay here. She'd manage it while she goes to school. AlkiSteel won't pay the utility bills much longer. We'd have to be careful. But with Walt's money, we should be okay until we figure out how to bring in enough funds for upkeep."

Crash could hear the words, but he wasn't really absorbing. It was hard to concentrate until they got to what he really needed to know.

"Sounds like a plan. But there's a lot you haven't mentioned."

She thought for a minute and cracked a tiny smile.

"Walt, when he was dying, said one thing I haven't forgotten. He said, 'It's not how much you leave behind, but how you leave it.' The fact that he helped so much—me, in particular—makes me want to do something for Flora and others like her. This is almost touchy-feely stuff, and you know how I hate that. But it happens."

She stopped. Crash waited for more. He still saw no opening for his own emotions. But there was another matter.

"I know you don't want to give up your father's tape, but maybe you should now. It could help the case against Tomson."

He expected anger, but instead got indecision in her reply.

"You're too trusting, you know. You think people's promises mean something. But they never do. What if Tomson weasels his way out of this? That tape is my insurance policy. Without it I have nothing."

He took his biggest chance.

"You have me."

She froze. Was she compressing for a sudden move?

He wanted to tell her he was not like the people who had disappointed and hurt her. But that would have to wait.

"Key, you need to hand over the tape. It's evidence now. Besides…"

He remembered a comment McHugh made.

"…with it, we may finally be able to find out what happened to your father."

He waited out a reply. Her shoulders relaxed. She looked away, as if she could see something beyond the walls.

"Under the engine of an old tractor behind the garage."

"You left it here? Dangerous, but gutsy, too. How'd you make sure the cassette wouldn't fall out?"

She actually laughed.

"A smart woman always carries duct tape."

His response had nothing to do with tape, duct or otherwise. He scooted closer. All practical questions flew out of his brain, and with them, the detachment that had protected him. He needed to know.

"When you say 'we'd have to be careful', what do you mean by 'we'? Just you and Flora?"

He saw a flash of her old reflex: Don't get too close, and don't you dare try to touch me. But it disappeared.

"Truth? I can't say for sure."

She studied him.

255

"You know I distrusted you along with the rest of the world. You asked a lot of questions. I hated your attention. Then I needed it when things went bad. Then I wondered about it when things got a little better. I thought a lot about that in the hospital. Could I stand you over time? Could you stand me? I missed you when I got back here, but I thought the best thing was to try a life completely without you."

"And how did that go?"

Her smile broadened, a contrast to the questing look that stayed in her eyes.

"I still don't know any better than I did."

He was locked into "I missed you" and had to say something.

"Do I get to know your real name?"

Her eyes darkened, then lit up with mischief.

"C-a-o-i-m-h-e, pronounced 'keevah'. Your turn. Was 'Crash' some sort of joke?"

"Sorta. My parents watched the movie Bull Durham on their first date. The main character's Crash Davis, and apparently I ran around crashing into a lot of things when I was little. The alternative would have been my real name, Ralph, because everyone said I looked like the kid in that other movie, you know, 'A Christmas Story'."

"No way!"

"Yeah, well, 'Crash' was no gift at MIT. You know, 'crash the computer'? I got a lot of that, but I still preferred it to 'Ralphie'."

They were both grinning. Her smile was different now, one that didn't hide the fact that she was hungry. For what? He thought he knew, and hoped with all his being that he was right.

DECEMBER 14

Key disentangled herself from Crash, one arm and leg at a time. She half remembered moving in closer all night long. Everything felt weird, like walking blindfolded—arms reaching forward for a handhold, one foot out front, then the next, feeling her way through it.

For now, she was wrapped in a blanket of lazy contentment. The things she needed to do today hadn't changed—go see Purgis and talk about the house, help Flora with community college registration. But the whole day seemed different somehow.

Then there was the part about getting close to someone, figuring out how he fit in, how they fit together. Trusting. That was the biggie. She wasn't any surer, in morning's light, that she was up to it; but she knew she was willing to try.

Crash was still dozing. The questions she was asking herself no longer felt like they belonged only to her.

She rolled out of bed and into a new world.

MARCH 4

"Thanks for coming. I thought it'd be good to get together and see where things stand. You know, put it all out there at once." Mc Hugh looked beyond them.

"Hope you enjoy our nice mountain weather. It's supposed to be clear, but rain's always possible this time of year. The venison barbeque'll be ready soon. For now, we can talk."

He stood aside to let them enter. Laura went first, then Crash and Key. McHugh looked at each of them as they passed. Gary, at the tail end, locked eyes with him and they exchanged a nod.

Gary guessed that McHugh hadn't furnished the room they entered. It had a peaceful feeling, with dusty, muted colors and neutral walls. Although the artwork and cushions added bright touches, they blended with rather than clashed with the room's harmonious tone.

The big cop himself was a changed man as he introduced his wife and daughter. He fumbled for words but showed visible pride. His wife Bebe, a tall, sturdy woman, cradled an infant and stood her distance as she offered a welcome. McHugh's eyes were full of tenderness.

Laura went to Bebe and began a low conversation. Gary knew that the two women had met before.

McHugh quickly reinstalled his professional neutrality.

"Bebe's got to feed the kid, and I've got to watch the venison roast. Might as well sit outside. It's a warm day, earlier than usual. But then, everything's changing around here, not just the weather."

Laura stayed inside with Bebe, and McHugh led them through an enclosed porch. A breeze passing through partially-opened windows carried smells of early spring and cooking meat.

In the yard, an unfinished wooden door lay across two sawhorses, making a simple table. Six folding chairs formed a ragged rectangle around it. McHugh took one of the chairs and motioned toward the others, then started right in.

"You've all been involved in a lot of heavy stuff. You must have questions, like about what's happened."

Key looked sour, then cracked a small smile.

"Ya think?"

Gary was getting used to Key's automatic sarcasm. But over the last weeks it seemed harder for her to keep it up. It didn't escape Gary how close she stood to Crash.

"So here's where we are on Tomson."

A couple of chairs hunched closer. McHugh looked directly at Key.

"Thanks for letting me have the tape. I listened to it before turning it over to the Shoreline DA. Nothing on it linked Tomson directly to your father's death, though there's no doubt in my mind he was behind it. We also have no proof that Tomson had anything to do with Walt Vickers' death, though I bet he was behind that too. The tape did prove Tomson's involvement in Gideon, and the DA can use that to strengthen their case."

McHugh waved his hand as if tossing something toward the distant peaks.

"Could be, though, that issues at Isadka will go away, as least as far as indicting Tomson goes. The state AG's decided to pursue just the murder and kidnapping charges for now."

Key broke in.

"When can I get the tape back?"

McHugh nodded.

"It may be months. But I did copy a relevant section."

He pulled out his phone and put it on speaker.

Static started, followed by voices that couldn't quite penetrate the noise. After a few seconds, a man's voice formed intelligible words, as if he'd moved closer to a microphone.

"…okay John, now you've got the whole picture…we all make money if… owners don't say they're acting on their own. Only consult with each other. I and my associates, especially Longcart…not involved…real arrangement stays out of the picture… and never known…get that?"

No mistaking Grant Tomson's voice. Someone else spoke, too soft to register. But it was clear that Tomson heard it because he broke in.

"…sure…good people, just don't know what's best for them… need experience…startup costs and management, those things… too hard for them to manage correctly."

The other voice interjected something, and Tomson came on again. Louder, angry.

"Careful, John. Use your head. Or your gut. What do you think'll happen to you and your family if the real project arrangement goes public?"

There was only crackling static until the second voice spoke again, matching Tomson in vehemence.

"Bastard."

Gary saw Key grab Crash's hand. Tears glistened.

"That's my dad."

McHugh gave her a long moment before going on.

"I guessed that. The audio guys say they have enough to identify Tomson's voice. But there's still the issue of the tape's admissibility..."

Key scrubbed the back of her hand across her eyes.

"What about Laura's recording?"

McHugh shook his head.

"Same thing. The DA's office is trying to get it admitted. Depends on the judge. We'll see."

Crash was shaking his head too.

"Sounds like there's a chance Tomson will get off entirely. That's not great news for us. He'll blame us for getting him in trouble. I'm sure not happy about having that threat hanging over my head for the rest of my life."

Gary had to agree. Tomson was like a cancer, infecting lives, destroying at will. McHugh nodded.

"Yeah, we're well aware, and law enforcement will do the best we can to look out for you. Meanwhile, we want to get Tomson for our own reasons, and we may have gotten a break. In an earlier case, a couple years ago, I was sure I had him nailed for his brother's death. But he tampered with evidence that related to a pair of old BMW bikes, so we didn't have enough to charge him."

A tight smile of grim satisfaction curled McHugh's lips.

"We were lucky you had the fight with Bowman over in Aggregate, Gary. Wait—I put that wrong. What I meant was it gave us a chance to question him. We've been looking at him for a long time for thefts and assaults all over central Washington."

"I don't see what that's got to do with Tomson. Is there any chance he'll beat the murder and kidnapping charges?"

McHugh shifted his position.

"I'll get back to Bowman in a minute. If you're looking for a definite answer, Gary, I can't oblige. We may get another crack at charging Tomson in his brother's death. But Clif's death and Tomson's attempt to drown Laura are the main focus now. The direction everything's going feels a lot more positive than the last time around."

"Tell us."

"Several important differences between the situation now and the earlier one involving his brother. This time Tomson's under indictment. Clif Lerman's autopsy confirmed a head wound from a heavy blow as the cause of death. We got a partial fingerprint off the automatic pistol we recovered from the water and confirmed that it's Tomson's. The medical examiner concluded that the butt of the gun could have been the object that caused Clif's head wound. It's still just circumstantial, but Bickers is eager to tell what she knows, and Groff, the logging foreman, will testify. On Laura, we've got her testimony about what happened up to the time she was pushed under water. Plus the tape."

"Can you continue to hold Tomson?"

"A judge granted bail along with a monitor until the trial. Tomson's lawyer is appealing the monitor, of course. A lot depends on how much political clout his people can drum up."

Crash broke in.

"This is the second time in eighteen months that Grant Tomson has been in the news connected with a crime. He'll have trouble in the PR area."

McHugh grunted.

"Damn right, and that's where Bowman comes in again. He's been involved with Tomson for a while, and he wants to bargain. He told us a lot—including where Grant's been holed up for the last months, farther east in the hills, in one of Bowman's houses, with a storage shed. Guess what was in the shed?"

"No clue."

"An old BMW bike. It's the missing one of a matched pair that was key to that earlier investigation. Bowman copped to being the one who hid the bike, and is willing to testify he hid it on Tomson's orders. So, goddammit, finally, we may be able to charge Tomson for his brother's death, too…"

Gary spoke into the pause.

"Excise the cancer, right?"

McHugh looked around and smiled. Then his face turned grim.

"I'm a cop, and I'll do my duty. But parts of this situation will never sit well with me. Bowman was okay before he went to Iraq. He came back wounded, and with PTSD. Didn't get much help from a country that used him, then discarded him. Tomson stepped in and used a physically and mentally wounded guy for his own purposes. Now we're thinking of charging the wounded warrior."

McHugh paused.

"Least we could do would be to have him re-evaluated at the VA hospital. He's there now, and we're waiting on the results before we charge him. He'll probably have to do time, but maybe there'll be some mitigation."

McHugh shook his head, and when he looked around again, the sadness had disappeared. Crash broke the silence.

"I'm curious. Tomson had a reputation for being smart and cagey. Why throw away all he had going over something as small as Isadka?"

McHugh shrugged.

"My guess? I've come to the conclusion that there's only two motives for crime. Need and greed. Tomson was all about greed, but he got ambushed by need for something—I don't know, for revenge or recognition? Something that took over in his mind. From my previous involvement with him, I know he had issues with his mother and brother. They're gone. So he picked other people as his target, maybe. I personally think his psychological needs became larger than his drive for money and business success. Lost his perspective, then his judgment. Went from ruthless to irrational. That's for a shrink to figure out. For me, it doesn't matter. He's guilty."

He brightened.

"Enough of that for now. Time to eat. Good thing Bebe didn't hear me. She's working on me to stop bringing cases home. Tomson can wait."

The others were moving toward the barbeque. Gary was about to follow when he saw McHugh beckon him over.

"I know marriage has been good for me. Gives you a different perspective. People said that, but I didn't believe it till it happened."

He shuffled his feet and turned to Gary.

"Laura's a good woman."

Nosiness wasn't in McHugh's makeup. He looked awkward, but Gary could tell he was trying to be helpful, so put aside his built-in inhibitions.

"Right about that. These past months weren't ideal for getting acquainted. We're working on that."

McHugh stayed impassive, though Gary would swear he was suppressing a smile.

Laura walked toward them and broke in.

"You two want to join the rest of us?"

McHugh and Bebe arranged platters of food on the makeshift table, and they all sat. Gary felt Laura's hand brush the back of his.

The ugly effects of the past would never vanish entirely. But those same events had brought them to this moment, and that was worth celebrating. Not just for its own sake—for the promise of more like it.

Gary raised his coffee cup. Quiet descended, and everyone turned toward him. He looked into each pair of eyes in turn and watched other looks lock around the table.

Words were not needed. Gary felt the bond that had formed. There was staying power in it.

8/11/16

From Clipcheck.com, your daily news summary
Prominent Seattle Businessman Sentenced
to Twelve Years in Prison
(Excerpted from *The Seattle Times*, July 17 at 10:30 AM)

Yesterday Superior Court Judge Walter Kraft surprised a packed courtroom with an announcement that the State of Washington would accept a plea bargain from businessman Grant Tomson. The agreement ends a trial that had already lasted three weeks, attracting widespread media attention.

In the agreement, Tomson will plead guilty to a charge of first degree manslaughter in the death of a former employee, Clifford Lerman, and will serve twelve years in prison. The manslaughter charge was a reduction from original charges of first degree murder and kidnapping. The sentence includes seven years on the manslaughter charge plus a mandatory five-year enhancement for being armed with a deadly weapon in the commission of the crime. The terms will run consecutively.

As part of the plea bargain, the State of Washington agreed to drop the concurrent charge of attempted murder of state employee Laura Dickens.

In separate trials relating to the same crimes, two other individuals—Curt Longcart, of Lynnwood, and Suzanne Bickers, of Seattle—were each sentenced to nine months in jail for second degree assault. Sentences will be served in a King County correctional facility.

Longcart and Bickers had originally been charged with kidnapping, but subsequently had that charge reduced in return for their testimony against Tomson.

Longcart's trial has attracted close media attention because of his well-known presence over the last two decades on late-night TV ads.

The State of Washington initially contemplated bringing other charges against Tomson. He was investigated for creating an illegal scheme that broke permitting regulations for a logging project at Isadka Valley. The Attorney General's office decided not to pursue that because no final contract had yet been signed and because of the greater seriousness of the kidnapping and murder charges.

Gary Seasons, a former Seattle Seahawk, was one of the individuals kidnapped by Tomson. When informed of the plea bargain, Seasons stated: "First, I'm glad that justice has been served and a man like Tomson will be locked away. But I hope the case also causes the State to tighten up supervision of logging projects so men like Tomson won't find it so easy to trick or force others to join in illegal schemes."

Related Story
Excerpted from *The Seattle Times*, July 9
State of Washington Settles Gideon Claims

The State of Washington and the logging company, TimberPartners, surprised court onlookers by announcing a proposal to settle claims by the residents of Gideon, Washington just before a trial on those claims was scheduled to begin.

The Gideon residents had sued for damages and other compensation after an earth slide below a logging project had destroyed homes and caused the death of dozens of people.

In the terms of the proposed settlement, the State of Washington will pay compensation of 40 million dollars and TimberPartners an additional ten million.

The payment will be made without admission of liability.

THANKS

For early reading and invaluable reactions:

Betsy Russell, Margaret Amory, Roger Page, Betsy Seaton.

For assistance on legal and sentencing issues:

John C. Steiger and Walter Schlotterbeck.

For advice on forestry issues:

Robert Ewing and Harry Wiant.

For editing and perspectives that go well beyond such a technical task:

Adam Finlay.

For everything in the publishing process, and prompt, reliable assistance:

Celeste Bennett

For a combination of all of the above and the patience to go with it:

Karen Neff, my indispensable partner.

CBN, 2/1/2017

CPSIA information can be obtained
at www.ICGtesting.com
Printed in the USA
FFOW03n1915040717
37389FF

9 781934 733936